A
Harlequin
Romance

OTHER

Harlequin Romances

by JAN ANDERSEN

CINNAMON HILL

by

JAN ANDERSEN

HARLEQUIN BOOKS   TORONTO
WINNIPEG

Original hard cover edition published in 1974
by Mills & Boon Limited.

© Jan Andersen 1974

SBN 373-01872-X

Harlequin edition published April 1975

Printed in Canada

CHAPTER ONE

The flight path of the great jet took it low over the triple-peaked mountain known as Les Trois Frères and down to skirt the eastern slopes of what many reckoned to be one of the most beautiful islands in the world.

To the girl with her nose pressed flat against the small window of the aircraft this was no exaggeration. Already the scattered islands rising out of the intense blue of the Indian Ocean seemed like a great curving belt studded with emeralds.

Two minutes later they touched down gracefully on the brand new runway, built out into the sea, and tucked between two tiny humpy islands. There was a brief glimpse of palms bending over a white gold beach before they turned and swung in front of the airport buildings.

Carrie craned forward for a first sight among the waiting crowd of Donald's thick thatch of wheat-coloured hair and the easy smile that first made her flip. Surely, she thought with a surge of disappointment, he must be here.

She stood for a moment in the arrival hall, surrounded by people, yet isolated from them, a small girl – too thin, some would have said – with tawny hair and eyes the colour of a fresh spring leaf. Only the extra observant would have noticed the expression in those eyes, as if their owner had known some great hurt or unhappiness that had left its mark in a special kind of wariness.

Five minutes later the crowd had thinned out and she was still there, not annoyed, because she knew there must be some good reason for Donald's absence, but a bit lost, and some of her initial exitement blurred by the tiredness of a long flight.

"Excuse me, can I help in any way?"

The owner of the voice was an unsmiling man with untidy hair a shade too long, and eyes hidden behind dark glasses. His hawk-like face reminded her of one of those Arabs she had remembered from her history books. He wore denim trousers and a dark blue tee-shirt while on his extraordinary brown feet were a pair of sandals. Obviously a local.

"Thank you," she said politely, "but I'm supposed to be met . . . or I could easily get a taxi. The island's not at all big, is it?"

"No." He had rather a flat, harsh voice. "Most of the hotels send out cars to pick up passengers."

"I'm not going to a hotel," she said, "it's a small farm called Cinnamon Hill. I don't quite know where as all my mail goes to a Post Office number, but . . ."

"Then you're going to the Bryants'," he said gruffly. "It's only about four miles. I'll drop you."

She hesitated. At home she was not in the habit of letting herself be picked up by strangers, particularly shabby ones, but then she wasn't at home, and this man obviously knew Donald, even if the way he watched and waited was oddly disturbing.

Even while she hesitated he raised a single eyebrow. "I could call out the airport manager to vouch for my credentials . . . or you may prefer to take a taxi. . . ."

"Oh, no," she said hastily, "I was only wondering whether to leave some sort of message here for Donald."

He flicked a finger for a porter to take her bags out to the car. "There's only one road," he said, "so if Donald is on his way, then we can't fail to meet him."

As he held the door open and she climbed into

6

For just a second Carrie looked from one man to the other and recognised the blazing antagonism in Donald's eyes. Then the stranger was nodding briefly to her, saying, "Enjoy your stay in the Seychelles, Miss Fleming," and with a rush of wheels against the hard crusty earth, he was gone.

When the car had disappeared from sight, she said slowly, "Donald, please . . . what's wrong? What have I done? He only offered me a lift from the airport."

"I know, I know. I'm sorry, it's just that I can't stand the fellow, and that you should arrive here, at my home, with him of all people, was just too much. I wanted to be there to greet you, and instead this damned old truck just died on me."

"Oh, Donald, you are silly, I'm here, aren't I? Isn't that all that matters?"

"Of course." Suddenly he was the old Donald, his eyes warm and loving, his arms tightly about her. "Oh God, it is good to see you, Carrie. Today has been the longest day I can remember . . . I haven't even asked you if you had a good flight."

"The last part was marvellous, but," she pulled a face, "it was a bit bumpy early this morning. I just can't believe I'm really here. And oh, to get into some cool clothes!"

"Then come in, Mother will have some tea on the go. There's one thing on this side of the island. We know precisely when the plane lands, so we can even have the kettle boiling at the right moment. Oh, here is Mother."

Carrie found herself shaking hands with a statuesque woman with a warm smile and grave eyes, whose large capable hands seemed to speak eloquently of their love for the soil.

"Welcome to Mahé, Carrie," she said in a voice whose faint accent Carrie did not recognise, and

9

bent forward to kiss the girl. "You must be tired, after all that flying. I think I preferred the days when we could only get here by boat. Come in and I'll take you to your room. You shall meet my husband when you've had a chance to wash and change, or rest if you wish. I don't suppose Donald has had a chance to tell you that he's broken his leg and will be out of action for some time. I hope." she went on, leading the way into a small but spotless bedroom furnished in white, "Donald has also explained that we live rather simply here. We had planned to build our new house down on the point, the other side of the road, but I suppose, as with farmers—or gardeners as we are now—the land comes first." She smiled again, a lovely smile that spoke of once great beauty. "And if there is anything you want, call. We have got out of the way of visitors, so we may be forgetful."

When she had gone, Carrie took a deep breath and sat down on the white wooden bed, trying to bridge the gap that was cold and frosty England of yesterday, and this jewel-like island of today—a thousand miles from anywhere, Donald had told her in London.

They had met on a blustering morning when he had come shivering into her office to keep an appointment with her boss who had only that morning gone down with 'flu. Mr. Jobling had phoned her and asked her to deal with 'this fellow from Africa' in his stead. "Take him out to lunch if you have to. He's come a long way to seek our advice."

But in the end it was Donald who took Carrie out to lunch, telling her she was the first pretty girl he had spoken to since landing in England a week ago, and then expounding to her his plans for setting up a specialist travel business in the Seychelles.

She confessed she had heard of the islands, of course, but had never actually seen them on any map.

"You wouldn't," he told her, "unless you have a magnifying glass. But one day everyone will have heard all about them. I shall see to that."

At their next meeting he told her about his parents who, though born in Seychelles, had spent the last thirty years in Kenya. Now, with land disappearing and long-term currency problems looming up, they had decided to return to their homeland. They had bought about twenty acres on Mahé, the main island, and were going to turn the place into the finest market garden one could imagine. "They're literally hacking the land out of the hillside—after taking down the palm trees first. It's a massive undertaking, but one thing you can say about my parents —they've got guts. I'm going back to lend a hand for a few months, or until they get on their feet, then I'm off to do my own thing."

As he talked about the place that had become his home Carrie found herself imagining it and the cluster of smaller islands that surrounded it, with such intriguing names as La Digue, where the only mode of transport was an ox cart, Praslin, with its famous valley where grew the largest coconuts in the world, Curieuse, once a leper colony, and many others. She listened, enchanted when he told her how much he would love to show her all these places —enchanted but disbelieving, because that kind of dream was impossible.

When the time for Donald's short leave was nearly over Carrie realised how much she was going to miss him. In those few weeks he had become a part of her life. More than that he had somehow acted as a barrier between herself and the recent past that had seemed so unbearable. It had been a long time since she had felt so . . . so protected

Three days before he left he phoned her at the

office and said: "Forgot to tell you, Carrie, it's glad rags for tonight. I've booked a show and then we're going to a very special supper."

"It sounds lovely, Donald." she said, trying to keep the hollow note from her voice. Special evenings meant farewells, and she hated farewells.

But in the end it was a wonderful evening, when everything went just right. It was impossible to feel miserable when the show turned out to be a hilarious comedy, the dinner one of the best—and probably the most expensive—she had ever had, and Donald's arm was round her nearly all the time, reminding her he was here by her side.

And the he said suddenly, his big hand over hers, "You know I'm flying off on Saturday, don't you?"

She nodded slowly, thumping back down to earth. "I've been trying not to think of it," she told him with great honesty.

"It doesn't have to end, you know."

Carrie put her head on one side. "What do you mean? You told me you had to go back. There are your parents, everything. . . ."

"Yes, I know. I do have to go back, but for *us* it doesn't have to end. I've been thinking about things for days now, Carrie, trying to find a way of telling you. I'm not awfully good with words. . . ."

She waited, still not understanding.

"I want you to marry me, Carrie," he burst out at last.

"Marry you?" she echoed. "But you've only known me a month!"

"Does it take a month to fall in love?" he said fiercely. "I think I fell in love with you that first day I walked into your office. You looked so lost so . . . sort of defenceless. I just knew I wanted to take care of you for the rest of my life. The point is, Carrie, do you love me?"

Carrie bent her head so that her hair fell like a burnished cloud over her face. When she looked up at him again her eyes were very soft, but her voice uncertain. "I don't know," she told him. "But I do know that when I'm with you I feel marvellously happy and safe, and the thought of you going all those thousands of miles is simply awful. When you kiss me, I *think* I'm in love with you, but to say that I'll marry you. . . ." her voice trailed away, before it gathered strength again to say: "For me, Donald, marriage is for keeps, I have to be sure. And how can I be sure when you're going so far away?"

"I've worked that out too, darling." He reached across and took both of her hands in his now. "Of course it's a lot to ask you to make up your mind just like that . . . but I can't let you go, Carrie. I am going to marry you, so as I can't stay in England, you'll have to come to me."

"To the Seychelles? But, Donald, that's impossible!"

"Why?" he demanded.

"I . . . I don't know, but it's not exactly like going to Spain, is it?"

"Other people do it." He grinned happily at her. "And they're not all rich! If you're worrying about the money, then I'm going to help with that. The package fare isn't expensive, especially if you're not using the hotel." When he saw the uncertainty still on her face he said urgently, "You've got to come, Carrie darling, it's the only way. . . ."

She had protested a little more, but only weakly, because she too wanted to be with him. She wanted to love and be loved, and as much as anything, she wanted to be part of a family again.

So here she was now, looking out towards the sea, feeling the faintest of breezes cool her cheeks. The only thing that was different was that she had insisted

13

on paying her own fare. That way they could start off on an even footing. But she had not liked that disturbing little scene out there just now. It had seemed so unlike Donald. Unless . . . she tapped a fingernail against her teeth. Unless Donald was *jealous*. Why she had not even liked the Brandon man. He was merely rather an off-hand stranger giving her a lift.

There was a knock at the door and Donald put his head round. "Hi, darling. . . ." He stopped. "Are you all right, you're just . . . sort of sitting there."

"I'm fine," she told him. "I suppose I was dreaming. I still can't believe I'm really here."

"Well, you are. You had me rattled for a moment. Mother says she's making a cup of tea in about half an hour. Will you come out for it, or would you like her to bring it to you?"

"I'll come out, of course. I can't miss a single moment now I'm here. Donald. . . ."

"Yes?"

"Who was that man who gave me a lift? Why were you so annoyed?"

The smile vanished from his face. "No one much," he said curtly. "Forget it. I'm sorry I got so het up."

"But you must tell me, otherwise I'll be wondering. And what happens if I come face to face with him somewhere?"

"That's most unlikely. Luckily, he's usually burrowing away in his bolt-hole. There's honestly nothing special about Jonas Brandon. He's merely a rich layabout I don't happen to like, who tries to play God. I'm surprised he even had the manners to offer you a lift . . . don't let's waste our time talking about him."

After she had showered and changed into a cotton dress, it was difficult for Carrie to believe she had been travelling for twelve hours. When she remarked on this to Mrs. Bryant, the older woman shook a finger and said, "It's a temporary feeling, Carrie, we all know. Take my advice and have an early night. Don't try to sit it out and then tomorrow . . well, tomorrow we can show off our beautiful island. Now, come and meet my husband and," she smiled, "if he grunts at you, don't take it personally. He's a man who's been active all his life and he doesn't take very kindly to sitting around."

She saw immediately which side of the family Donald took after. Oliver Bryant was a big man, almost bigger than his son, with weathered skin and the same shock of hair, but peppered with grey. Even though he was propped up in bed she could see there was not an ounce of spare flesh on him, only muscle. He shook hands firmly and seemed to glower at Carrie from under bushy eyebrows. But though his voice was gruff, his welcome was kindly.

"So you're the girl Donald never stops talking about." He looked her up and down. "We'll have to lend you a bit of our sun—and put some flesh on you. Don't they feed you properly in England these days?"

Carrie blushed. "I'm afraid I've always been thin, and as to the sun . . . well, it is winter at home."

"I know. Don't take too much notice of me. I haven't been to England for ten years or more—and then I didn't stop long. I felt too shut in. Too many people."

"Then you must have stayed too long in London," Carrie protestedly loyally. "Most of England is beautiful."

"Hmm—wait till young Donald takes you round the island, then I'll ask you again!"

Still smiling, Carrie came back, "I expect . . . I know I'll love it here, but it won't make me turn against England. It's just . . . well, different."

Oliver Bryant burst into a deep roar of laughter

that seemed to come right up from the tips of his toes. "I like you, Carrie, we're going to have some good arguments while you're here. Just wish I could give you the grand tour myself. I'd show you the places that Donald doesn't even know exist."

"Oliver," his wife put in reprovingly, "give poor Carrie a chance to catch her breath and have a cup of tea." She squinted across the verandah. "She's brought good luck, I think. By the looks of it we're going to have a shower of rain tonight, which is just what my plants need if they're not to die."

Carrie woke to the dazzling blue of a sky without a single wisp of cloud and a sun that seemed to fill the whole room. But it had rained, for she remembered waking briefly and hearing it drumming on the roof and for a moment had thought she was back in Enland.

Now she lay for a moment, luxuriating in her new surroundings, watching in delight as two bright emerald green lizards chased each other across the far wall, tails flicking, tongues darting, until they disappeared through the ventilator hole, probably to continue the game elsewhere.

It was too good to lie here. The thought of that sea, the new world to explore, made her throw back the sheet and dress as quickly as possible.

But to her surprise there was no one in the house except a young and smiling maid who did not seem to be able to speak much English. So Carrie went outside to see if she could find either Donald or his mother.

Only now, in the full light of the morning, with the damp steaming from the ground, did she see what an impossible task the Bryants had set themselves. Most of the planting had to be done on a slope, for the narrow shelf that surrounded the island

16

could not have extended here for more than a hundred yards or so. While much of the ground was under cultivation there was an even larger portion that was just rough earth, scattered with the stumps of palm trees.

She heard the sound of voices above her and made her way towards them. Donald and his mother were standing gazing at the crumpled remains of a small building.

"What's happened?" she asked. "Oh, what's happened?"

"You might say," Donald said bitterly, "that luck isn't running our way just now. This is our new hen house. We were expecting a hundred young chicks to be delivered tomorrow, but now. . . ." He paused his hands despairingly through his thick hair.

"It was a tree," his mother finished for him. "The rain must have loosened its roots, and sent it straight down the hill on to the hen-house. I think," she turned to Donald, "it might be as well not to tell your father about this until we've found some sort of solution."

Donald was stil staring at the rubble. "It's like taking one step forward and two back. I'm beginning to think you and Father are crazy after all."

"Nonsense," Jane Bryant said sharply. "Think how much worse it would have been if the chicks had actually arrived." And after the moment's appalled silence at the thought of that tragedy, she went on, "Now let us be practical instead of crying over spilt milk. What's the first thing that needs doing?"

"The first thing I should be doing," Donald pointed out, "is the day's deliveries, but I can't do that without the truck—or at least without the small van. And that's at the garage. . . ." He scratched his head "On the other hand, I must stay here and get something done about this."

17

Carrie touched his arm. "Please, Donald, there must be something I can do to help. I can drive," she pointed out. "Could I deliver or something?"

Donald regarded her doubtfully. "You're here on holiday——" he started.

"And a marvellous holiday I'll have," she snorted, "lying on the beach, thinking about all this happening here! Please, I want to help." She turned to his mother and appealed to her.

Jane Bryant thought for a moment, her beautiful skin furrowed in concentration. "All right," she said at last, "if you want to deliver, then you shall deliver, but first we have to get you in to Victoria to pick up the little van at the garage."

Just twenty minutes later, after Carrie had gulped down a cup of tea and enjoyed her first taste of pawpaw, she was waiting in the road outside to pick up the first of the local mini-buses that were the main mode of transport running up and down the road to Victoria. Jane had told her she would recognise the buses by the strange, sometimes funny names the drivers painted on them. So when "Catch-me-if-you-can" came round the corner, Carrie flagged it down.

It was fairly full, but everyone pushed up to make room for her. She was immediately conscious of two things—first how nearly all of the passengers smiled at her. In fact they seemed to smile and laugh all the time. A happy people, someone had told her in England, and how right that was! The other thing was the range of colour of the skins, from the darkest ebony to a creamy white, and none of them, she guessed, was European.

She watched eagerly as they broke new ground, past the airport again and then along the winding road that became steadily more populated until down the last stretch of road and there was Victoria.

The clock tower—focal point of probably the

18

smallest capital in the world—was easily found, and from there Carrie, following Jane's directions, made her way to the garage. The car, it seemed, was ready, but as they were not expecting Mrs. Bryant until later in the morning, would she please be happy to wait for about fifteen minutes.

So Carrie wandered back to the centre, trying to keep out of the sun, to explore the narrow back streets, lined with Indian and Chinese shops with wares piled up outside and cars hooting as they vied with pedestrians for a passage.

She peered into the home industries shop, enchanted by the shells and the basketwork and the brightly coloured straw hats, and wished she had more time to go in and explore further, but for the moment the the only important thing was to get back to Cinnamon Hill.

As she approached the garage again the first thing she noticed was a tall girl who managed to look elegant even though she was wearing old jeans and a cotton shirt, leaning on the white van as though she knew it well.

She turned in surprise as Carrie approached to put her hand on the door. Carrie had a quick impression of dark glossy hair and the kind of face that would have been a photographer's dream before the other girl said, "I was expecting Donald Bryant . . . isn't he with you?"

Carrie shook her head. "No, I'm collecting the car for him. There's been a bit of a storm which has done some damage at Cinnamon Hill, so he stayed to cope with it. Is . . . is there any message I can give him?"

"Yes, I suppose you could." She paused, as if assessing Carrie as a suitable messenger. "I wanted to ask him to double up on my order for green peppers. I tried to phone, but the lines were down as usual. You must be the girl he was expecting from

England."

"That's right," Carrie nodded. "I'm Caroline Fleming. Who shall I saw wanted the peppers?"

"Just say Margo. He'll know. . . . Donald and I have known each other for a long time." She smiled, and it seemed to Carrie there was no guile in that smile. She was merely stating a fact. Then she raised a hand. "I must dash . . . get Donald to bring you over to my place some time. We're supposed to have one of the best positions on the island."

Carrie watched her stroll, with a model's walk, over to a long low scarlet sports car. For some reason her mouth felt dry and when she looked up at the sky there was the smallest of fluffy clouds on the horizon.

CHAPTER TWO

On that first day of her holiday Carrie was pitched in at the deep end and found herself enjoying it. While she was eager to discover some of the beauties of the island she was even more determined to become a useful part of the Bryant family. After all, it was more than likely they would become her in-laws

So when she returned with the car she was provided with a map by Mrs. Bryant, who explained:

"It's difficult to get lost, Carrie, because there is really only one road that goes most of the way round the island and five roads across. At the moment we supply our fruit and vegetables to three of the smaller hotels and those are clearly marked . . . see?" She pointed to where she had written the names clearly. All of them were on the coast road so they would be easy to spot.

Donald was stacking the back of the van with wooden trays piled high with pumpkins, bananas, onions, paw-paws peppers and aubergines, all clearly labelled with their destinations, when Carrie said, "Oh, by the way, I met a girl called Margo at the garage. She asked if you could double the order for green peppers. Is . . . is she at one of the hotels?"

Carrie sensed that Donald hesitated just a moment, and then he pushed in the tray he was carrying, so that she did not see his face as he replied, "Yes, the Casuarina, it's the last one on your route."

"And the prettiest on the island," Mrs. Bryant put in. "If I were you, Carrie, I'd take a swimming suit with you. It's a perfect place for a bathe. Margo St Clair would be only too pleased."

"No!" There was that sharp note back in Donald's voice. "I would rather Carrie got back here, then I can take her for a swim after lunch."

"Very well, dear," Mrs. Bryant shrugged easily. "I just thought it would be a break for Carrie...."

"Maybe, but *I* want to be able to take Carrie for her first swim. I don't particularly like the idea of her going off like this on her own, her first day anyway, but I suppose I have no alternative." He turned to Carrie and his voice was full of concern as he said, "You will take care, won't you, darling? I know there isn't much traffic on the roads, but the driving here isn't of a particularly high standard."

"At least it's on the left," Carrie laughed. "Of course I'll take care. I've even driven a mini-van like this, so that makes it doubly easy. *And* I'll take you up on that swim this afternoon!"

The first two hotels were within a few miles of each other, well established, small places where she was made welcome and questioned about Mr. Bryant's broken leg and then asked to describe the damage the rain had done. It was quite obvious that this was a small close-knit community and even more so that everyone held Mr. and Mrs. Bryant in high regard.

For her last call she had to cross the island, over the low ridge of hills behind Victoria. She found the way without difficulty, then dropped down to find herself running alongside the beach of Beau Vallon ... the place that Jonas Brandon had said attracted all the tourists. She could see why; it was a beautiful, palm-fringed beach without a coral reef, so the water flowed, deep and blue. For just a moment she wished she had brought a swim-suit, but then thought loyally that it would be much more fun to swim with Donald for the first time.

She found the Casuarina Hotel without much difficulty. It was perched on a rocky promontory looking down into a tiny secluded bay, with a small islet cutting it into two separate sections.

Carrie parked the car and walked round to the side to get someone to help her unload.

"Well,well, so we meet again." Margo St Clair was standing there, her huge sunglasses pushed to the back of her head. "They're making you work hard on your first day here. No, no . . ."she waved a hand, "leave all that to the boys. I was just about to have a drink of lime. Would you like a glass?"

"I'd love some." Carrie followed her through the hotel and out again to a terrace overlooking the sea, where she stopped short.

"Oh," she said, for some reason slightly flustered, "it's you again."

Jonas Brandon unfolded himself from his chair and held one out for her opposite him. "Yes," he said, "it's I. You've rested, I hope, Miss Fleming?"

"Thank you, yes." She could not stop the wary note creeping into her voice and she did not sit down immediately.

Margo looked from one to the other. "So you two have met. For a so-called recluse, Jonas, you were fairly quick off the mark."

"We met by accident," Carrie said stiffly. "Mr. Brandon was kind enough to give me a lift from the airport."

Since she could hardly go on hovering there, and the tray of fresh lime juice was just arriving, Carrie sat down. "I mustn't stop," she said quickly to Margo."I imagine there'll be other jobs when I get back."

"I thought you were on holiday," Jonas Brandon said lazily, and she was forced either to look into his hawk-like face, or be deliberately rude.

"I am, but it hasn't taken me long to learn how easily things can go wrong at Cinnamon Hill. Last night the new chicken house was smashed. . . ."

"I'm sorry about that," was his comment, "but I told them long ago that it was the wrong piece of land."

"I don't suppose," Carrie returned evenly, "they had a lot of choice." She was just beginning to see why Donald and this man were not on the same wavelength. For some inexplicable reason she even felt vaguely disloyal sitting down at the same table as him. So she drank down the last of the delicious lime, saying that she must be on her way. She smiled at Margo. "The Bryants will be thinking I'm shirking on my first day out."

"You could have a swim if you wanted," Margo said. "Look down there, the beach is tiny, but it's the most secluded on the island."

Carrie walked to the edge of the terrace and followed the direction of her gaze, down into the bay, where she could now see the semi-cirle of golden beach. It looked marvellously inviting, but. . . .

"I'd love to," she shook her head regretfully, "but if I could come some other time. . . . Donald did say you have a most beautiful position here, but it really is like a small paradise—and blissfully quiet."

"Sometimes too quiet," Margo pulled a face. "Down there," she pointed to the other side of the islet, "is one of the only small natural harbours on Mahé. No coral reef and deep water. Perfect for a private marina, only I can't do it."

"What's stopping you?" Carrie said curiously.

"He is." And Margo jerked her head goodhumouredly towards Jonas.

For the first time Carrie noticed the full glint of gold on her hostess's left hand, and she spoke her thoughts aloud "Oh," she said, "I didn't realise you two were married."

Margo gave a shout of laughter, and as she threw her head back, Carrie could almost see that wonderful smile on the cover of a magazine. She flushed. "I'm sorry, what have I said?"

It was Jonas Brandon who answered. "Nothing unusual, Miss Fleming, except my sister-in law is particularly flattered."

"At least," retorted Margo, "I'm too polite to speak my real thoughts aloud. My monkish brother-in-law would rather stay on his desert island for ever than be married to me, *and* not be afraid to say it. You could say that we have a delicate but uneasy relationship—eh, Jonas?" He said nothing, so she turned to Carrie, who was embarrassed at being the cause of these home truths. "Fortunately, like his beloved brush warbler, he's a rare visitor to the Casuarina. Isn't that right, Jonas?"

From the man still seated on the edge of the terrace the only reply was an enigmatic smile. To Carrie he nodded briefly. "Goodbye, Miss Fleming. Don't take too much notice of Margo. My bark is worse than my bite."

Margo saw her to the car. "I'm sorry you couldn't stay, but Donald must bring you over to dinner. I like to think that my cuisine is also one of the best on the island. And please," she touched Carrie's arm lightly, "don't feel you intruded in any way. Jonas and I always argue, it's part of our way of letting off steam. He's enormously shy and doesn't like people, but for me, they're my life."

Carrie was thoughtful as she drove back to Cinnamon Hill, wondering and curious about the two people she had left behind at the hotel. She longed to ask Donald, but instinctively knew she must wait for the right moment. All that mattered just now was that she was here, with Donald, at last.

He was waiting for her as she drove into the clearing and her pulse quickened at the way he turned and waved at her.

As she got out of the van he said, "You've just got time to go inside, grab your swimming things, and then we're off."

"But what about. . . ."

He put a finger over her lips. "Off, my girl, and don't push your luck. Mother has made up a huge picnic for us and says I have to take you out for a couple of hours, or you'll be catching the next plane home." He grinned. "*I* know you won't, but I'm also too wise to look a gift horse in the mouth."

Carrie needed no bidding. Within ten minutes she was out again and, with Donald at the wheel this time, they were bumping down the track and on to the road, heading away from the airport

He turned towards her. "Happy, darling?"

"Oh yes. It's difficult to believe I'm really here, and yet after only a few hours I feel as if I've been here for ever. Isn't that strange?"

"Not at all," he said promptly, "merely the effect the Seychelles have on everyone. Didn't you know they were called 'The Isles of Love'?"

"No." She turned to him and smiled. "Is that really true?"

"It certainly is. Mind you," he slowed down to pass a couple of children, each carrying fish almost as big as themselves, "the origin of that description doesn't do the island much credit."

"Why?"

"Because we have a very high rate of illegitimacy. Locals tend to take 'love' very literally."

" Well, they all seem so happy."

"They are," he assured her. "You rarely see a sad Seychellois. Give him some fish and some rice and a roof over his head, and he's a truly contented man." He added ruefully, "I wish I could say the same for myself."

Within a few more minutes Donald had swung

26

off the coast road and was heading through a huge coconut plantation across the other side of the island.

"Where are we going?" she asked happily.

"To one of my favourite beaches. Perhaps not the most perfect—that would take too long, so we must save it up for another day. Oh, Carrie, there was going to be so much to show you, so many places to take you, and now with Dad laid up the way he is . . . it's not going to be all that easy."

"Then we'll have to do just what we can," she said softly. "If I don't know what I've missed, then I won't really have missed it, will I?"

"I suppose not. And anyway, one day soon you'll be coming out for good." He paused. "You will, won't you, Carrie?"

"I. . . ." Carrie wanted to say 'Yes, of course I will' but the cautious streak that was part of her nature, held her back. "Don't rush me, please, Donald . . . it would be all too easy to say yes, but when I do, I want to be absolutely certain."

He shrugged goodhumouredly. "I know, darling, I shouldn't have pressed you yet. There's plenty more time, let's just make the most of each day. And," he pulled off the narrow road on to a hard sandy space, "here we are."

As Carrie followed him through the gap in the trees and found herself on a tropical beach for the first time, she felt it was rather like treading where no man had trodden before. She tossed off her sandals and felt the hot golden sand trickle between her toes. The beach was quite straight and empty, with not even a single footprint to ruffle its smoothness, with the pale emerald of the Indian Ocean surging against its edge.

"Come on," Donald held out his hand. "We'll go to my special bit of shade," and he led her to where a huge tree overhung the beach."

27

"What is it?" asked Carrie, looking up at where its branches bowed gracefully, providing the perfect shelter from a sun that was blazingly hot.

"A takamaka tree. You'll find plenty of them all round the beaches of Mahé. This one, though, is my private bit of property. Now, do you want to swim or eat first?"

"Swim! What do you think?"

Within a minute she had dived into the undergrowth and slipped on her brand new bikini, the colour of freshly picked lemons, then hand in hand the two of them raced into the water.

She came up gasping. Never had she been in such clear water. Why, she could even see the reflections of the sun on the sandy bottom.

"Five minutes only," Donald yelled at her. "This sun will be lethal on your first day, even in water." So reluctantly, just when she was beginning to think she could float on its surface for ever, she allowed him to hustle her out.

Carrie rubbed herself briefly with a towel and then ran her hands and arms through the fine sand. "It really is like paradise, isn't it?" she said at last.

"It is now that you're here. Come here, Carrie, do you realise you've been here nearly twenty-four hours and I haven't even kissed you properly yet." Obediently she went into his arms and as his lips touched hers she thought, surely there can be no greater happiness than this.

Afterwards, as they lay on the sand watching the tiny land crabs dig their holes and disappear at the slightest scent of danger, Carrie said, "It can't be easy for your parents to make a go of Cinnamon Hill. Can't they get more help?"

He shook his head. "They can't afford more than a couple of full-time hands—besides, they're difficult to find now. Most of the labour is being em-

28

ployed by the construction companies who are building the hotels and improving the roads. The Seychellois don't like working harder than they have to."

"At least," Carrie said lazily, "in this sort of climate things must grow easily."

"That, unfortunately," Donald said, turning to kiss the end of her nose, "is where you're wrong. There's virtually no topsoil on this island because once the palm trees are removed the rain washes it away, leaving only gravel. So practically nothing grows easily. You'll see that when we have a proper tour of Cinnamon Hill when we get back. Root crops are hopeless . . . things like potatoes and turnips have to be imported. All I can hope is that Dad's work pays off one day. I think he would be more encouraged if he actually owned the land."

"Doesn't he?" Carrie was surprised.

"I mean," he said, and there was a taut note in his voice, "Mr. Jonas Brandon won't let him buy."

"Oh, I see." She did not really see at all, but at least there was now a glimmer as to the reason for Donald's hostility towards the other man. Again, she held back further questions, not wanting to spoil the perfect mood of the afternoon.

Reluctantly, after they had eaten the chicken pie Mrs. Bryant had packed for them, together with the stubby bananas and a huge mango, they packed up to go back. Carrie felt almost drowned in sunshine, and her flesh tingled from the salt.

By the time the early tropical darkness fell that day, she felt almost bewildered by the amount her senses had tried to take in. Wanting to help Mrs. Bryant, she had offered her services and found there was at least something useful she could do, by helping with the watering that was a daily chore that could not at all be mechanised.

29

She learned to distinguish the new tender pepper plants and the sturdy aubergines. She picked her first bananas and learned with amazement that the paw-paw trees, if carefully nurtured, could bear fruit in about six months. And then Mrs. Bryant took her up to her own special domain, the nursery.

"I'd like the time to grow more flowers," she said wistfully, pointing out the young orchids in pink and pale purple and creamy yellow growing strongly under their roof of palm leaves. "Oh, there are plenty of hibiscus and frangipani and other ornamental shrubs, but not enough flowers that people can pick and buy to put in vases. I want to change all that." She sighed. "But it will take time." She tapped the girl on the shoulder. "There's Donald calling you. I think you'll find him up at the pig unit—up that path, almost to the top."

So Carrie saw how the Bryants had made a start with about twenty pigs and learned that it would be the manure from them that would help to provide compost for the gravelly soil. Even to her inexperienced eyes it seemed to be a huge undertaking.

"Right," said Donald, checking the last of the sties, "that's it for the day. As soon as I've washed, we'll take our drinks down to the point, just across the road. We actually do own that bit of land."

It was really, she discovered later, just a fairly small spit of land on which were a few trees and a tumbledown boathouse, but there was just enough sand to provide a patch for sunbathing and the small rocky promontory acted as a natural landing stage for the boat to be launched.

Sitting there, watching the moonlight cast its strange, dappled shadows, Carrie could hear the strange whirring noise of the crickets and in the distance a cock crowed.

She sipped her drink and turned to Donald. "This

is just what I believed a tropical island at night would be like. Can we swim here?"

"Bathe, but not really swim. The water this side of the reef is too shallow. I only wish it wasn't, I might then have a chance of building my marina here. As it is, if I start up the travel business in the way I want to there's really only one other place on the island."

In the shimmering half darkness he was suddenly very still. "At the Casuarina Hotel, I suppose," she said softly.

He turned quickly to her. "How did you know?"

"Margo showed it to me, but told me her brother-in-law doesn't approve."

"I told you he liked to play God." He seemed to be speaking through clenched teeth.

"Tell me, Donald, I'll have to know sooner or later, does Margo own the hotel, or does he?"

"Oh, he does, of course. About five years ago his younger brother James met Margo when she came out here on a big modelling job. I never met him, but I'm told he was quite a different kettle of fish."

So she is a model, Carrie thought. At least I was right about that.

". . . Well, they fell in love and got married. James had only been running the hotel a short time, it was leased from his brother. I believe they wanted to buy but couldn't raise the money. Anyway, James was killed in a flying accident about three years ago and Margo decided to keep on the hotel. She's made a great success of it: it's become known as one of the best eating places on the island and she only has room for about a dozen staying guests. But still he keeps an iron hand on what she does with the land. I think he would like to own half the Seychelles if he could, gives him a sense of power or something. As long as he and humanity can stay apart. I reckon that's why he won't sell Cinnamon Hill to my parents."

Carrie stared at him. "You mean Jonas Brandon is your landlord?"

"Too right he is!"

"So that's what he meant this morning. . . ." Carrie's voice trailed away and in the silence that followed the noise of the crickets seemed louder than ever.

At last Donald said in that strange terse voice she was beginning to recognise whenever Jonas Brandon's name was mentioned, "What do you mean Carrie—'this morning'? It was yesterday he gave you a lift, wasn't it?"

"Of course it was, Donald, but—well, he happened to be at the Casuarina when I delivered the things to Margo."

"Then you shouldn't have stayed. I made my feelings about him quite clear yesterday."

"How could I?" Carrie flared angry at his unreasonable attack. "I didn't know he was the until Margo brought me round to the terrace. What was I expected to say?—'Donald disapproves of you, so I must go'—I just wish I'd been born with second sight," she added bitterly, "then something would have told me to refuse his lift yesterday."

"No, I suppose you couldn't have done that," Donald growled. Then after a short pause he said, "Why didn't you tell me he was at the Casuarina?"

Carrie sighed. "First, because I don't think it was important enough, and secondly that if I'd told you at lunch time today—the only chance I've had—then it would have spoilt everything. You seem to have got an unreasonable dislike for this man."

Donald stood up. He looked enormous beside her. "And I suppose *you* like him!"

For just a moment Carrie stared at him, totally unbelieving, then she turned and ran across the road up the path and into her room, when she sat for a moment, shaking.

Do all people in love have rows? she thought. It was the first time she and Donald had quarrelled and over something that, to her, was totally unimportant.

After a time, when she had collected herself, she washed her face and went to see if she could help Mrs. Bryant with the meal, but she was hustled out of the kitchen. "At least," Jane Bryant told her, "if we don't have much help in the garden, then we do have some indoors. Ginette is a wonderful cook, so you just sit down. It will be ready in about ten minutes."

So Carrie went and sat on the wide verandah and it was there that Donald found her. He stood and looked at her for a moment, then she ran into his arms and he scooped her up. "Oh, Carrie darling, I'm sorry, I don't know what I was thinking of. I suppose I'm just a bit down with all the work to do here and with little chance of getting myself launched. It's just getting on my nerves, I suppose." So Carrie smiled and the stupid quarrel, that had shaken them both, was over.

During the following morning, after Carrie had done some chores and been hustled away by Mrs. Bryant, she decided to put on her swim-suit and start serious work on her sun-tan. So she collected a book, a towel and some oil and crossed the road to the boathouse.

She had been lying there for some time when she heard a voice with an unmistakable Scots accent say, "Hello, I think you must be Carrie," and looked up to see a thin girl with a freckled skin standing above her. She jumped to her feet and said, "Yes, I'm Carrie. And you. . . ."

"Welcome to Mahé." The other girl held out her

hand. "I'm Sally Raymond. Bill and I are next-door neighbours of the Bryants. You can just about see our bungalow through the trees, right over there. We heard you'd arrived and wanted to make ourselves known to you."

Carrie smiled. "That's nice of you. I'm just trying to get rid of some of this awful English whiteness."

"Well, don't rush it," Sally warned, " this sun is much stronger than you think. I've just been over to tell Donald that Bill and I are going to take the boat to do some goggling. We suggested to Donald as he's obviously rushed off his feet that you might like to come."

Carrie's eyes lit up. "It sounds marvellous. You mean we would go on the reef?"

"That's right. Bill's crazy about it and is starting to do some underwater photography. I just like to have a swim and watch the fish. So would you like to come?" She glanced at her watch. "We'll have to catch the tide, so that means leaving in about half an hour. Can you make it?"

"You bet I can!"

As Carrie gathered her things together and made a dash across the road the other girl called after her, "Bring a hat, and something to cover your shoulders —oh yes, and some rubber shoes."

Carrie found Donald up working on the now partly repaired hen-house. He was scowling and only when she called his name did he turn and smile.

"You're sure you don't mind my going with Sally Raymond? I can easily stay and help if you want me to, but you did *force* me to go and sunbathe, didn't you?" she said breathlessly.

Carrie saw by the barest second's hesitation that deep down he did mind her going. Probably he wanted to take her himself . . . but then he said, "Of

34

course you must go, Sally and Bill are a marvellous couple. I expect Mother will be inviting them in any day now."

So she reached up and kissed him lightly. "Thank you, darling. I'll bring you back a beautiful shell."

"You can't!" he called after her. "It's against the law!"

In an odd sort of way Bill Raymond was a little bit like his wife, reddish hair and a freckled face and a Scots accent. But Carrie liked them both immediately. As soon as they had pushed out from the make-shift landing stage, he explained that he and Sally had a sort of part share in Donald's boat, helping with the expenses so that they could use it whenever they liked—which wasn't often, apparently, because Bill did not often get a day off and when he did they usually had their five-year-old son Simon demanding their attention. But today he had gone off to play with a friend across the island.

It took about fifteen minutes to reach the heart of the reef and here Bill dropped anchor and handed Carrie a mask. "Don't splash about," he warned her, "or the fish will vanish, just paddle about and keep your face under the surface. It's just a question of getting used to breathing." Then he helped the two girls over the side.

If Carrie could have gasped aloud she would have done. She had many times read and seen photographs of the beauties that lay beneath the ocean, but she had never dared to believe she would see those for herself. The coral was like a landscape of its own, hilly, then flat, all shapes and sizes, yellow and bright blue, darkening into mysterious-looking caves. Then there were the fish, first a bright yellow striped one, then a shoal of electric blue.

She could have lazed there for ever, but Sally tapped her on the back, reminding her of the sun, so she climbed back into the boat and then it was Bill's turn to dive.

The two girls sat and talked, with Sally amused at Carrie's ecstasy over all she was seeing.

"Have you lived here long?" Carrie asked.

"More than two years. Bill's on a three-year tour. He works for one of the construction companies, but he hopes we'll be able to come back for another three years. By that time we'll need to be thinking seriously about Simon's education, so I expect we'll go back to Scotland. But we love it here." Her eyes lit up. "I know, we're having a barbecue up in the hills at the end of the week. Will you and Donald come? We could introduce you to some people and they'll all be delighted to hear news from home. Our world is quite a small one. We were all thrilled when we heard Donald had met someone from England. Up till then we'd thought. . . ." she stopped abruptly.

Carrie went on rubbing furiously at her hair. "What did you think?" she said in a muffled voice.

"Oh . . . oh, nothing."

Carrie said with her usual honesty, "If it was someone else, I don't mind. You see, Donald and I have really only known each other for about a month, apart from letters, so I didn't expect him to have led a blameless existence."

"No, of course not." Sally brightened. "Donald could always be relied on to be a spare man at any party. There was safety in numbers, he would tell all the girls."

Instinctively Carrie knew she was trying to cover up. There *had* been someone special in Donald's life, and presumably if Sally was so evasive, that girl was still somewhere in the Seychelles.

Carrie found herself talking non-stop about what she had seen on the reef that evening, and after supper Mr. Bryant found her some books to read on identification of the fish and the coral she had seen. He then insisted that she should look at his remarkable collection of shells. It was a happy evening, and without difficulty Carrie knew she was fitting into the ways of the family. It was that which pleased her as much as anything.

The following morning, after breakfast, she saw signs of the van being piled up again with produce.

"Deliveries?" she said cheerfully. "Shall I do them today?"

Donald put down the tray of melons he was carrying. "No, not today," he said.

"Why not?" she came back innocently. "You keep saying you have so much work. At least it's something I seem to be able to do."

"No," he said again. "If anyone does deliveries, we do them together."

She felt a tiny twist in the pit of her stomach. Perhaps she should have left well alone, but it was not her nature to accept something she could not understand.

She went round to the back of the van and faced Donald, a small girl, with fire in those green eyes. But when she spoke her voice was very quiet.

"It's something to do with the Casuarina," she said at last, "isn't it? You didn't question me about any of the other hotels. For some reason you don't want me to go there. I really believe this man Jonas Brandon is becoming an obsession with you."

"Carrie, you're talking nonsense, it's simply that I don't think you should go wandering off on your own. That first day was an emergency, but today isn't, so we'll go together."

But Carrie knew they were facing something quite important, something they must come to terms with if their love was to mean anything.

"To me," she said, "love means absolute trust,

37

and I don't think you trust me yet, Donald. It would be better if you did your deliveries alone today. I prefer to go and help your mother." And very straight and stiff, she walked away from him, into the house.

CHAPTER THREE

When Donald had gone Carrie immediately regretted her outburst. They had so little time together that to waste it quarrelling was unforgivable. Besides, she ought to have guessed that he must be under great strain. She wandered inside and tried to help Mrs. Bryant, but she was engaged in the planting of some special seeds, so after watching for a while Carrie gathered up her swimming things and wandered across the road to the beach.

For a while she hugged her knees and looked out to the calm still sea and thought about yesterday. She needed to get away and think about things on her own. She had always been like this at home, liking to work everything out for herself.

The boat, moored there, slapping gently back and forwards with the tide, looked tempting. She had handled a small boat like this with an outboard motor many times when she used to spend her holidays on the Helford River in Cornwall.

It took only a few moments to throw in her towel and shoes. If the engine was a tricky one she would give up the whole idea, but with one pull on the cord it burst into roaring life, so she headed out across the shallow lagoon following the well-defined passage Bill Raymond had taken yesterday.

There was no chance of diving off the boat today of course, but the hazy scattering of islands not so far away looked so romantic there was surely no reason why she should not beach somewhere safe in shore and have a proper swim. Because she was so intent on steering straight ahead of her she did not see the grey ominous clouds piling up over the mountains directly behind her. All she was aware of was the breeze was suddenly cooler and the leaden air marvellously fresh. I won't go far, she told herself, just to where she could tell by the intense blue of the water that the sea bed suddenly dropped away from the coral.

When I get back, Carrie decided, I'll apologise to Donald and tell him that if we both have secrets then we should tell them now. That way there'll be no need for doubt or distrust.

When the first cloud crossed the sun it was like a curtain coming down, and she looked behind her in faint surprise that turned to alarm as she saw more huge black clouds gathering and heard the rumble of thunder. And then the first drops of rain fell.

Just as she had read about many times she could not really imagine, Carrie had read about tropical rain. If she had thought about it at all she would have assumed it would be something like a brief but heavy downpour at home. But what happened now was not in the least like that. The rain swept down from the mountains in a great torrent, hitting the water with a noise like hailstones. Within a minute she was drenched from head to toe, added to which the spray from the now wind-whipped water seemed to be attacking her from the front. Worse than anything, however, was the realisation that she had lost all sense of direction, for she and the boat were enclosed in an all-enveloping grey blanket.

Carrie bit back a small sob. Crying would be useless, for there was no one to hear. Whatever happened now she had brought upon herself. But she still, for all her pretence of bravery, could not control the violent chattering of her teeth.

The engine was still chugging on. Was it better to go forward or back? Back meant finding her way through the coral reef, and forward . . . well, that was into the unknown, and yet it had seemed to her when she last looked that the outline of the nearest island had not seemed far away. In any case, as she realised, with an appalling dawning of truth, after ten minutes of this, with her head bent to keep the worst of the whipping rain and wind from her eyes she had not the faintest idea which was forward or back—she could be going in a complete semi-circle for all she knew.

Shutting her eyes—for she was little worse off that way—Carrie tried to summon to her imagination the picture of the islands that were in sight of Cinnamon Hill. Was there any chance, if she kept on going, that she would simply head towards the open sea? Reluctantly, she admitted to herself that there was indeed.

After only a complete day on Mahé she could hardly expect to know her islands. There was Cerf and St Anne and several smaller ones, but those were all in a group. Towards the east, as far as she could remember, there was not very much.

Now the sea was beginning to roughen considerably, no longer the warm friend, but a grey, white-capped enemy. Her sailing lore from those Cornish holidays was not very extensive, but at least she knew she must keep the prow heading into the waves, for once the boat was broadside on, it could tip her over. That meant, Carrie knew, that she had to keep the engine going at all costs. But how much fuel was there in the tank? She and the Raymonds had been out for a couple of hours yesterday and they certainly had not filled up with petrol on their return, so it could mean there was very little indeed.

It must have been not long after this awful thought that she realised that the rain was easing off. The heavy blanket had become a thin grey veil, and the downpour a steady drizzle. But with the easing of the rain, the wind was rising and the little boat was starting to rock unpleasantly. And then the unexpected happened, the worst thing of all. There was a hideous grinding noise, which for a few seconds she could not identify, then she saw the water bubbling into the bottom of the boat and knew either she was near land, or she had merely crossed the coral reef.

Carrie started to call out, to shout, but only the noise of the engine and the sea came back to her. In desperation she tried to plug the hole with her towel and then with some old canvas that was in the locker, but while it slowed the tide, it certainly did not stop it, for first her feet were in water, and then her ankles, and she knew with certainty that the boat was sinking. When the engine spluttered and died and there was a different kind of silence, she gave herself up to the knowledge that there was no hope of rescue and she started to weep, quiet choking tears of despair. 'Oh, Donald,' was all she could think of, 'and I never even had time to tell you I was sorry'

When Carrie was finally tipped into the sea, strangely a little calmer now, she allowed herself to float, to be carried where the tide took her. The water was suddenly a little warmer and gentler too, as if in her last moments it was cradling her to her final rest.

The feeling of something soft under her toes only half penetrated through her consciousness, but the will to live must have been buried deep within her, for she turned on to her stomach and started to swim. When a larger and stronger wave than before pitched her on to some sort of land, something made her crawl on until she finally pitched into real unconsciousness. There were voices in her head and a burning sensation all over her body, and the only thing that Carrie could think of was that it was not too bad to die after all.

After a little while, although she still could not find the strength to open her eyes she realised that the voices were talking quite clearly and therefore they could not be inside her head. The language she could not recognise, except oddly enough there was a sprinkling of English and French words. She turned to one side and burrowed her cheek in the hot soft sand and must have passed out again, because the next time she came round she heard a distinctly English voice say, "Good God!" and then she was picked up without very much ceremony, carried some distance and laid down on some sort of hard bed. There were no voices and she was out of the sun, and yet she still burned all over. It was all a dream, it must have been a dream, and she could not stop small bitter tears escaping to run down her cheeks.

"I don't want to die!" she cried out, and the voice that replied, vaguely familiar, as if from a distant past, replied:

"You're not going to die. You're quite safe, although God knows you don't deserve to be." And someone wiped away the tears.

When Carrie finally opened her eyes, she knew she was alive, but it was pitch dark and she thought for a moment that though death had not come, blindness had, and she stifled the cry that came to her lips. A few minutes later vague outlines took shape and a shaft of silvery light through a window told her that it was night and what she was seeing was moonlight.

But where on earth was she? She struggled to sit up and found that her body and head were aching. The room, if it was a room, was very small, but more than that she could not tell.

Carrie felt rather than heard the door open and knew that someone was standing there. She opened

43

her eyes again and saw the figure blocking the open doorway.

Taking a deep breath, and knowing she could put off the moment of truth no longer, she said in a shaky voice, "Please, who's there and . . . and where am I?"

There was a moment's silence, then a voice came from the motionless figure. "You are on a privately owned island, called Tern Island, Miss Fleming, and how you managed to make your way here I have yet to find out. Do you feel well enough to tell me, or should I send you back the way you came?"

She swallowed. Now she really must be dreaming. Was this man going to plague the whole of her stay in the Seychelles?

"Mr. Brandon," she said at last. "Are you really Jonas Brandon?"

"I am indeed." And she heard a match strike and a few seconds later there was the glow of a kerosene lamp which he put on a rough stool just inside the door.

When her eyes were accustomed to the light, she looked about her and decided she was in some sort of hut. In it was the narrow bed on which she lay, a table on which was an old-fashioned bowl and jug for washing, a kind of seaman's box, and a few hooks on the wall. The place could not have been more than about ten feet square.

"Well," he said, "I'm waiting. I'm presuming you didn't swim all the way from Mahé, and yet anyone there knows that my privacy here is absolute. I allow no one on Tern Island unless specifically invited. And that, I may say, is a very rare occurrence."

The annoyance that had been festering in Carrie now blazed into outright anger. She pulled herself into a sitting position and cried at him, "I didn't invite myself to your wretched island, I didn't even know it was here. If it hadn't been here I suppose I

44

would have drowned by now—and I suppose, as far as you're concerned, that would be a much better thing!"

"Don't be stupid," he snapped. "The spit of land where you were found by my boys is well known to locals as a perfect place for swimming. Who suggested that you, too, might try it? Who brought you here?"

"I'm trying to tell you," she yelled, "no one brought me here. How could I have heard about your beastly bit of beach after two days?" In a quieter more, controlled voice, she went on, "I took the Bryants' boat out, meaning to potter round the shore near Cinnamon Hill, or go across to the nearest island. The rainstorm came up and I lost my way completely. The next thing was that the boat was holed on the coral and it sank. I didn't even swim here—the tide threw me up on the beach. At least I suppose that's what happened. I don't remember." But even that memory was enough, and before she could stop herself, she had burst into tears.

He seemed to stand there for a long time. She didn't know whether he was watching her, mocking her, or merely bored with her.

"I see," he said at last. "Then you were quite right. Had Tern Island not been here, you would almost certainly have drowned. There's nothing between here and Frigate Island, and since we cover only eighty acres, you could easily have missed us. When did you leave Mahé?" he finished abruptly.

"This morning. Mid-morning," she whispered.

"Then you'll be hungry. I'm afraid our fare is very simple, but I'll bring you something."

"You needn't bother," she started to say, but he was already gone, and besides, even as she spoke she realised she was hungry.

It was only as her mind started to function norm-

45

ally again that she realised the thin towelling robe she was wearing was not part of her survival kit. Quite obviously it belonged to him, since the sleeves were far too long. She had only been wearing a bikini . . . horror of horrors, she discovered she was not even wearing that now. Had it come off in the water, or . . . she did not know which prospect was the worst to contemplate.

Why, of all people's beaches to be thrown up on, did it have to be one belonging to Jonas Brandon? She could just see Donald's expression of disbelief. Three times in two days was too much of a coincidence. She almost believed it was herself.

Donald! The Bryants! She clutched the robe to her and climbed out of bed, only to sit on the edge, feeling distinctly wobbly.

"Please," she said, as he appeared again in the doorway, "what about Mr. and Mrs. Bryant—and Donald? They'll see the boat gone and will be wondering what on earth has happened to me. I must let them know." She started to scrabble to her feet.

A hand on her shoulder pushed her gently back on to the bed. "Drink this, Miss Fleming, I'll explain our position."

Obediently she sipped at the mug he proffered and discovered she was drinking surprisingly tasty soup. She felt its warmth flow right through her, and with the warmth came renewed strength.

"I'm very sorry, Miss Fleming, but at the moment there's nothing I can do about the Bryants, much as I regret it."

"Nothing?" she echoed. "But there must be something! Oh, I know you won't have telephones here, but you must be in some sort of contact with Mahé."

"No contact at all. That's why I came here."

She stared at him in the eerie glow of the light. That unsmiling face was serious and the rather hard

46

It's the only thing I can find in which you won't be totally swamped. The sun is going to be strong today; you'll need some covering. Did you sleep well?"

She nodded.

Wearing nothing but an old faded pair of trousers, Jonas Brandon did not look so forbidding, or even so angry, this morning. His black hair was ruffled and untidy and in his hands he carried a workmanlike notepad.

"The only thing I'm afraid I can't offer you is something for your feet, but most of the island is fairly soft sand, so you shouldn't come to much harm."

"Thank you."

"Oh, and there is something else," She waited, already deciding that although she was an unwanted guest, she did not really have to put up with the merciless lash of his tongue.

"I want to apologise," he said curtly. "I spoke without thinking last night. My somewhat antisocial ways tend to lead me into saying things I don't always mean. You had a very unpleasant experience yesterday and while I can't relieve your worries about letting the Bryants know where you are I can at least make your brief stay on Tern Island as pleasant as possible." Suddenly he smiled and she had a first glimpse of the man behind the mask. "Am I forgiven?"

"Of course." She too found herself relaxing, as if she, she had been tensing herself to carry on their private war. "I too must apologise in a way," she said slowly. "I did an extraordinarily silly thing yesterday taking the boat out without telling anyone. I don't know what came over me. I really am lucky to be alive at all."

"Yes," he said gravely, "I think you probably are. And" and the brisk note was back in his voice, "breakfast will be in about fifteen minutes. I've been

50

mouth was even faintly disturbed. Perhaps, after all, he actually cared just a little.

"Then you must have a boat," she retorted. "You can't be that far in miles from Mahé."

"That's quite true, but it's just your bad luck that you arrived at this precise moment. Normally I have two boats here. It was on the larger one I went to Mahé three days ago, to have the engine serviced. The reason why I was at the airport was to pick up a spare part. When I returned, I discovered that one of my boys had got a badly infected foot, so I sent him to the doctor. With a bit of luck the pirogue will be back tomorrow, or at the very latest the following morning. Our only other hope is that we attract the attention of some fishing boat tomorrow, but it will to be one with a shallow draught, or it will never get over the coral."

"So you really are on your own desert island," she said in a hollow voice.

"That's right. It's not to everyone's taste, but it is to mine. Ah, here's Johnny with a little fried fish, it's all we can rustle up in an emergency, I'm afraid." He passed her a plate on which there was a slice of most delicious-looking fish. Carrie half wished she could tell him she was not hungry, but the smell was too tempting.

"I suggest," he went on, "when you've had that you get a good night's rest. I'll get Johnny to bring you along some fresh water for washing—not too much, I'm afraid, as water is always in short supply. And there's a privy about twenty yards down the path outside. You'll find a torch beside the bed."

Carrie looked down at herself and remembered she was wearing only a robe. "My swim-suit," she said in a low voice, "what happened to that? It's . . . It's all I've got."

"Yes, I must apologise for removing it. I had little

47

alternative."

Carrie knew she went a fiery red and prayed he could not see in this light. "What do you mean?" she cried. "You could at least have left me my ... my...."

"Dignity?" he finished for her.

"Yes," she hurled at him, "my dignity!"

"Miss Fleming, when my boys found you on the beach, I have no idea how long you'd been there, but the bad weather had been cleared for some time and you were lying in the full sun. I have no doubt you'll feel the after-effects of sunburn tomorrow, and if I hadn't removed your swim-suit, I think you would have been in worse pain from the dried salt. I assure you I have better things to do than gloat over what had to be done."

"Then what am I supposed to sleep in?" she said between her teeth.

"The buff, I should think. Again, I have to tell you," he said in a grave voice, but now she did suspect he was mocking her, "that there's no one on this island except myself and the three boys that are left. None of us will disturb you—you have my word for that."

When he had gone she lay for a moment, fuming, then there was a knock at the door and the boy who had brought the fish beamed politely and placed a jug of water on the floor.

Carrie washed herself as best she could and dried on the towelling robe. She would like to have brushed her teeth, but she was certainly not going to search for anyone for that. But on the table that served as a washstand there was a comb and above it was a small mirror, so at least she did her best to pull her tangled hair into some sort of order. Only then did it occur to her that this was his room. What had Donald called Jonas Brandon? 'A rich layabout?' Well, there were few enough signs of his wealth here on Tern Island.

48

Her visit to the privy by torchlight was a fle affair, as she ran with some nervousness alon path. She was beginning to think she was th one on the island, such was the silence.

Back in the hut, Carrie hesitated a momen flung off the robe and dived under the singl and its thin cover. It was hot, but not the stifl of Mahé. She wondered briefly where Jonas was sleeping since she had obviously turned of his quarters, but then, before she could t further, she had plunged into a deep, sleep.

It was the sound of birds that awoke h vellously rich, trilling melody that was miliar. She lay and listened to it, wonder pure notes of happiness. Then she real a sort of background chorus she could he sound of other birds and beyond th boom of surf on the sand.

In spite of her experience yesterda surprisingly well, although her skin w back and shoulders where the sun ha How long, she wondered, had she lai day before they found her? Proba never know, since after the first rai lost all count of time.

She sat up and pulled the towel her, then, cautiously, she climbed opened the mesh door. To her am that the hut was actually on the be a few yards from the creaming sur stopped to imagine what a deser like, this was probably it.

On a small block of wood outs bikini, neatly folded, and benea shirt. She picked it up and look

"I should put it on if I were

49

checking on the water situation and after yesterday's rain there should be enough for a quick shower. Come, and I'll show you what our routine is."

She followed him about a hundred yards along the beach to where there was a spit of white-gold sand where it shelved so sharply into the aquamaine sea, it was almost possible to dive from its end.

"This," he said, "is where you landed yesterday. Perhaps you can now understand why people for miles around want to swim here?"

She nodded. "Yes, I can, even having seen several of the beautiful beaches on Mahé. But why don't you want people to swim here—to keep it all for yourself?"

"No, even I am not quite as selfish as that. Tern Island, as you'll see later, is a bird sanctuary, and while I can swim quietly and I can ask you to do so, I can hardly expect to control ordinary holidaymakers who want to enjoy themselves. So it's better to say they can't swim. If it makes you feel any better, the same rule applied on Cousin Island which is a reserve owned by the International Council for Bird Preservation and locally under the jurisdiction of the government. But on Tern, I am master. Now, as I was saying, we usually have a swim here, and then there behind you is a tank of water."

Carrie looked round and saw the tank, supported by branches of two trees and under a shady roof of palm leaves.

"You pull that string and the water comes out of the bucket below. It's a ramshackle affair, but it seems to work. Oh, and…" now there was a real glint of humour in his eyes . . ."if you don't want to sit around in your wet swim-suit all the morning, I can promise you there'll be no one to disturb you. Two of the boys are at the far end of the island, Johnny is preparing breakfast, and I shall be in the laboratory

51

until you come. This is a very small community, but we've learned to respect each other's privacy."

She watched him go, noticing with a faint surprise that he walked with an oddly stiff gait. Perhaps he too had an infected foot but had not bothered to go to the doctor.

The thought was pushed to the back of her mind as she turned to contemplate the brilliant, tempting blue of the water. Well, if she stood here thinking about rights or wrongs much longer, she would never be able to make up her mind so, without more ado, she tossed off the wrap and plunged into the cool, clear depths.

It was like diving into the centre of a jewel, pale and translucent, with only the soft sand underfoot to refect sky and bright sunlight. But she did not linger, for natural shyness forced her up the spit of beach to enjoy that quick burst of fresh water over her body, washing away the salt, before she dived into the robe and ran back to the hut.

A few minutes later, feeling sparkling fresh, she put the shirt round her shoulders and made her way through the border of the casuarina trees to where in a shaded clearing a table was set up with rough wooden benches at either side.

Jonas Brandon rose to his feet. "Enjoy your swim?"

"Yes, thank you." Then teasingly, she added, "It was *almost* worth being shipwrecked for that!"

"Now you know why I keep the hordes out!" There was a moment's silence. "Turn around, Miss Fleming . . . no, I think I must call you Caroline. On Tern Island we're very informal, as you see."

"I'm usually called Carrie," she said shyly.

"Carrie, then, it's a nicely old-fashioned name. Turn around."

She did not know why she should have obeyed

him, but she did.

"Hmm, aren't you sore?"

"Yes . . . yes, I suppose I am a little, but there's been too much else to think about to worry about a bit of sunburn."

"Seychelles sunburn is not something easily forgotten, but we have our own remedy. Johnny," he called to the wide-eyed smiling boy who was standing patiently by, waiting to serve breakfast, "bring some of our special salve."

When the boy returned with a small pot, Jonas Brandon ordered her to sit down on the bench, and then proceeded to rub whatever was in the pot all over her back.

She started to rise in protest, but like last night he pushed her back. "This is no time for prudery, Carrie, you should have got used to our down-to-earth ways by now—you've been here for more than twelve hours."

Think of him as a doctor, she told herself, feeling the strong sure strokes across her back and shoulders, it's all it means to either of us, but it was still difficult to shut her mind from Donald's face, and the rage—justified, she knew—if he realised where she was and what was being done.

Already the sting was disappearing and her back felt cooler.

"Right," he said, "put the shirt on and we'll have breakfast."

As she pulled it over her head she said in a muffled voice, "Do you always give everyone orders?"

With raised eyebrows he answered, "No, not always and not to everyone. But I think you wanted me to tell you what to do—didn't you?"

In the small silence that followed she said in her coolest voice, "Didn't you say something about breakfast?"

Fortunately, the odd mood that had sprung up between them was broken, and he was passing her the dish of fresh mangoes and bananas and explaining that the round slab in the centre of the table was goat's cheese, which he normally ate with whole-meal biscuits.

"Bread, I'm afraid," he told her, "is a luxury on Tern Island. We have it when a boat comes in or when Johnny chooses to make some, which isn't very often, because flour is scarce too."

The goat's cheese was surprisingly good, washed down with strong tea, which he told her came from the huge tea estate on the high terraces round Morne Blanc, one of the higher peaks in the centre of Mahé.

"Do you know anything about birds?" he said in his odd abrupt way.

"Not very much," she confessed, "but more than some people, perhaps. My father was very keen on bird-watching, particularly sea-birds, and when I was a child he used to take me with him sometimes. That was in Cornwall. I remember he was one of the few lucky people to find a nest belonging to the rare Cornish chough and he was so excited you'd have thought he'd found a diamond mine at the bottom of the garden." Her face clouded. "But that was a long time ago. He died, you see, and I've lived mostly in cities since then. But I still love to see and hear the birds. There was one this morning that woke me up. It was so beautiful . . . I thought for a moment I was dreaming."

"That was a brush warbler, or sometimes we call it the *petit merle des isles*. To say that it's rare is an understatement. The only place it has ever bred before is Cousin Island, where there are about thirty pairs; but now we have three pairs, so Johnny and I and the other boys watch over them like a lot of clucking old hens."

54

He drained the last of his tea and bit into the large juicy mango, with all the relish of a schoolboy. Then he turned to her and said: "At about this time every morning, I do my 'round' of the island, checking on the nests, and on other minor changes that could have taken place from the previous day. It's a small part of my routine, but one I enjoy. Would like to come?"

She met those dark eyes and that oddly appraising look and decided he really was trying to make up for yesterday.

"Yes," she said, "I'd like that very much."

CHAPTER FOUR

For the next hour and a half Carrie found herself totally absorbed, so much so that when Jonas Brandon told her how long they had been walking she could hardly believe him.

The tour first took them on a well defined path that completely circled the small island, mostly under the trees, but still blisteringly hot, although somehow it did not worry her.

Everywhere there were birds and as they made their quiet way along the sandy path it seemed to Carrie she was in a giant aviary. He pointed out to her the tropic bird with its long white tail streamers, the small green-throated sunbird whose noisy trilling song seemed to come from everywhere, and the small sparrow-like creature he called a toc-toc, which he proudly claimed to have started breeding on the island in the past couple of years.

This man who guided her with such authority and who pointed out so many things with obvious pleasure was quite different from the one who had treated her so carelessly last night. She wondered what had made him put up this barrier against society.

"Please," she said suddenly. "you've hurt your leg, I noticed it this morning. Should you really be taking me round like this?"

"Since I hurt it five years ago," he said harshly, "I can hardly go on pampering myself."

"I'm sorry," she said, taken aback by the ferocity of his reply, "I didn't mean to intrude. I just thought . . ."

"Yes, I know, you 'just thought' I needed propping up, like everyone else."

"I haven't the least idea what everyone else

56

thought," she tossed back at him, "I was merely try-ing to be human—which you seem to find great diffi-culty in being." She stopped and looked at him. "Do you really suspect the motives of people you meet?"

To her complete surprise he replied, "I think I do. It's a difficult habit to shake off. I suppose I should thank you for reminding me of it."

Carrie opened her mouth and closed it again. She really did not begin to understand this extraordinary man.

He had walked slightly ahead. "Look, Carrie, come and look at this fellow."

What was left of her anger died instantly, and she knelt to where he was pointing into the hollow of a tree.

"Oh, isn't he beautiful?" she breathed, looking in at the large fluffy white chick nesting there, who gazed out at them both with huge, mournful eyes.

"You see," said Jonas, reaching in and picking the bird up to let it rest in the palm of his hand, "he's learned complete trust in humans, just as all the other birds here have. This island is for them, we're only here on sufferance, to make sure no harm comes to them. Take him, Carrie."

"May I?" Very gingerly, afraid she would be the exception to his rule, she allowed the snow-white bird to nestle warmly on her hand. "Why, you're right," she cried in delight. "It seems so impossible."

Even more impossible, she discovered, were the graceful fairy terns, after whom the island was named. They were everywhere, their gleaming white feathers showing up against the feathery branches of the casuarina trees.

"They only lay one egg," Jonas told her, "and look what crazy places they choose—with no nest it's as likely to be on a branch of a tree as anywhere else. See, there's one—that chick can't have been hatched for more than a day or two." And she found herself looking up at a tiny, fluffy little thing perched precariously on a twig, hardly more than a couple of inches thick.

"But how does it balance?" Carrie asked, amazed.

"By its claws. It will stay there until the time comes to fly away. It has staying power, something we could all do with. Come on, there's a lot more to see yet."

Their half way point proved to be a small hill in the centre of the island whose pinnacle was a huge granite boulder. From here, under the great wheeling wings of the black frigate birds they could see all round them.

"That's Mahé, is it?" Carrie pointed.

"Yes."

"It looks so near. I almost feel I could swim."

"It's four miles. A long way without a powered boat."

Some of her pleasure from the morning's excursion died when she thought again of Donald and his parents.

"They'll think I've drowned, won't they?" she said soberly.

"I hope not, though, I only wish I could offer you some reassurance. It has been suggested that at least I should be in radio contact, but isolation has been a balm to me. I didn't think of anything like this happening, because, apart from Margo, I've never had visitors who've stayed more than a few hours. Besides, there's always been one boat in working order. Your arrival is part of a series of unfortunate coincidences. I wish I could make a suggestion, but I can't. When you do return, however, I will call on Mrs. Bryant and offer my own explanation."

"No!" She had spoken forcefully, without thinking, and colour rushed into her cheeks. "I'm sorry, I didn't really mean that, but I think it would be better if you left it to me. After all, this was all my fault."

"I understand," he said dryly, "but *Mrs.* Bryant and I have always been on excellent terms. It's unfortunate that . . ." He stopped. "No, it's better that I don't try to influence you. I presume you're going to marry Donald Bryant?" Swerving off on a tangent, he shot the question at her, his manner changing to his earlier abrupt one.

"We haven't finally decided yet, that's why I came over here for a holiday, but . . . yes, I think we will marry."

He stood up, glancing at his watch. "It's time I was back at the lab. I'll show you our small colony of giant tortoises. If you're interested in them, then you can come back on your own and watch them." He moved away from her, down the hill, and once again she wondered how the first rift had opened between him and Donald.

The tortoises were in a walled pen, something over an acre in size. She had never believed such animals could be so large—like creatures from *Gulliver's Travels*. For the moment they were not moving, their heads were tucked under those massive shells.

"They're asleep," he told her. "As I said, you can come back if you like, it's worth spending half an hour here, they're lumbering but entertaining creatures. That one," he tapped it lightly with his foot, "is reckoned to be somewhere around a hundred and fifty years old."

"A hundred and fifty!" she repeated, stunned.

"Oh, yes, some of those on Aldabra—the only place in the world where you'll find them wild in any numbers—are getting on for a couple of centuries."

When they reached the hut again, Johnny was waiting with a bottle of Coke for her. Carefully dusting the sand off the bench under the trees, he stood aside for her to sit down.

"You have seen the tortoises?" he asked, his ebony face split with that broad beam.

"Yes, I have seen the tortoises," she told him.

"Miss Fleming is returning to have a look at them," Jonas said, and turning to her, "Johnny is in charge of the pen. I think he loves the tortoises more than he loves me."

Johnny looked at his employer in horror, not seeing the joke at all. "No, Master, that is not true. I do not . . .".

"I know, Johnny," His master gave him a friendly punch across the bare shoulders. "It was my way of telling Miss Fleming how good you are with the beasts."

"Oh, yes, I am good with them." He was cheerful again. "They will do anything I want."

Carrie met Jonas's amused glance and they both smiled, a natural smile born of a small joke recognised and understood. Then he moved away.

"I must get down to my other chores, Carrie. Can you swim or amuse yourself until lunch time?"

"Yes, of course." She paused. "Have you any paper you can spare me?"

"I think so. Come along to the lab and I'll see what I can find."

She followed him along to the other hut, and looked curiously round as she followed him inside. About twice as large as the sleeping hut, it was definitely a room designed for work, with charts and photographs all over the wall, files everywhere, and a sink and lab bench taking up one wall.

"A notebook, would that do?"

"Something larger if you have it. I'd like to make one or two sketches," she explained shyly.

"Then why didn't you say so?" and from under a

60

pile of books he produced a drawing block from which he tore the top few pages.

"Thank you." She paused in the doorway. "Is there anywhere I shouldn't go?"

"No, not really, but you would be advised not to stray too far from the paths. Partly because you have no shoes and partly because you don't know where the birds are nesting. And here," he reached to a hook and tossed her an old khaki hat, "take this, just in case you find yourself in the sun."

The rest of that morning raced by for Carrie. She backtracked to the tortoises, watching their slow clumsy movements for a while before she returned to where the baby chick nested in the tree, sitting in exactly the same position as a couple of hours ago.

Within the next hour the pad was covered with drawings, the tern chicks on the branches, the sunbird, and others whose names she did not know. She discovered bright green lizards, and larger brown ones that merged into the colour of the dry earth and strange red and blue crabs that darted in and out of their holes. It was a wild and beautiful place and she longed for the facility to put all she saw down on paper. For it was fairly obvious she would never be returning here again. One visit on sufferance, yes, but another, invited, never.

She did not hear Jonas arrive until he had almost reached the spot where she was perched on a granite boulder, the funny brown hat tipped over her eyes.

He watched her for a moment, then said, "You have a feeling for movement. Have you had lessons?"

"Only evening classes," she said ruefully. "I'll never be good enough to do more than draw for pleasure. But I have a project to do while I'm here." And she found herself explaining quite naturally that she was entering a competition in England and had hoped to find a subject in the Seychelles that interested her, because here she would have the time to draw.

"I suppose," she finished, "there are birds on Mahé."

"Oh, yes, but whether they'll sit long enough for you to draw them is another matter." There was a moment's silence. "You can come back some time if you like."

"Could I?" Her face lit up, and then she remembered, "Oh, but . . . I don't think that would be possible."

"Donald can bring you. You could perhaps explain that I'm not luring you into my lair. There are no ulterior motives."

"*I* know that." She suddenly realised that she did, but whether she would ever explain to Donald was quite another matter. "Anyway," she said brightly, "since I'm a sort of prisoner, I can carry on this afternoon."

He shook his head. "No, not this afternoon. Your release has arrived, that's what I've come to tell you. There's a boat on a deep fishing trip anchored some way out. In another hour the tide will be up and they're sending their small craft to pick you up."

"Oh . . . oh, how marvellous!" But for some ridiculous reason she was faintly disappointed. She would have like to spend the rest of the day here.

She stood up, carefully putting the pad together. "Then I must be ready, mustn't I? Although," she tried to laugh, "I can hardly collect my belongings."

"You'd better keep the shirt," he said curtly. "Four miles of sunburn won't do that back any good. You can leave it with Margo and I'll pick it up when I'm next across. Come on, Johnny is getting lunch. At least you can report to the Bryants that Tern Island has fed you to the best of its ability."

Throughout the meal of fish and fruit she was

quiet, worrying now about facing Donald, apologising to his parents. Somehow, these last twenty-four hours *had* seemed like being on a desert island and, surprisingly, a not unpleasant experience.

From where they were sitting she could see the boat that had come to 'rescue' her tossing gently on the rippling sea, not more than three hundred yards off shore. As she drained the last of her coffee she saw them lower a dinghy, then a man start to row towards Tern Island.

"Are you always going to live here, Jonas?" Because she was leaving she felt bold enough to ask this man the question that had been on her lips all the morning. "I mean, don't you ever want to join the . . . the world?"

He looked at her from under hooded lids, his dark arched brows furrowed in a deep frown.

"I doubt it, at least not in the way you mean. I've had many years of living with the world, as you call it, and not all was a particularly pleasant experience."

"Don't you want to have any . . . any sort of *job*?" she persisted. It was out of the realms of her experience that any man should spend all his days pottering about a tiny island studying the birds, however admirable it was to preserve them.

"There are jobs and jobs," he said enigmatically. "I believe some folk on the mainland call me something between a playboy and a layabout."

Carrie ducked her head, trying to hide the swift colour in her cheeks. That was exactly what Donald had called him.

"Ah, I see that shaft went home," he said, not without humour, "but I can't please everyone. At the moment it seems more important to be true to oneself. One day perhaps you'll learn that. You're very young, Carrie, aren't you?"

"I'm twenty," she said sturdily, "and used to coping for myself."

"I've no doubt," he returned, "but experience has something to do with life, not age. Don't worry," and suddenly he smiled that rare smile, "I've no intention of becoming a complete drop-out. In order to appreciate this place I have to leave it sometimes. That's why I make my forays to the mainland. And I'm not ashamed to say, I do like my creature comforts occasionally, and the odd ritzy meal. Oh, yes, and I do have a few friends who don't totally disapprove of me. It's a good thing to have friends, Carrie, remember that. Now," he stood up awkwardly, "I think you'd better go." He held out his hand. "I've no doubt we'll meet again."

His clasp was cool and firm, but when she met his eyes, she caught an odd expression in them, just for a fleeting moment, as if . . . as if this bravado at living the solitary spartan life masked a real loneliness. And then it was gone, and she knew she must have imagined it.

The people on the boat turned out to be a couple of American tourists who had indeed been on a deep fishing trip and come back with a huge marlin. They were father and son, with the open cheerful way of many of their countrymen. The son, who introduced himself as Harvey Mercer, whistled appreciatively as he hauled her aboard from the dinghy.

"I say, we didn't realise we were giving a mermaid a lift, did we, Dad? We'd have come for you ourselves. Looks a crazy little island, that—all birds, they say, and a hermit who lives there, Oh, gee, I'm sorry, I suppose you were visting."

"No, not exactly. I got sort of stuck in the storm yesterday and took refuge there."

"Then you were lucky, wasn't she, Dad? We heard on the grapevine that some girl was actually lost

64

yesterday, drowned, so they say. . . ." He stopped, caught sight of her face, and grinned. "Say, it wasn't you by any chance?"

She nodded. "That's why I haven't got any shoes, and why I'm in this borrowed shirt."

"Well! Well, there's a story to tell the folks at the hotel. We're at the Reef, where are you staying?"

"With friends."

They landed her fifteen minutes later, with warm invitations to come along to the Reef for a drink, or a meal. She'd be very welcome. And Carrie knew they meant it. But just at this moment, she had other things on her mind. She stepped ashore on the rough landing stage below Cinnamon Hill, waved her hosts goodbye, then turned to cross the road and meet the Bryants.

She was half way up the rutted track, picking her way painfully over the stones and dried earth that tore at her bare feet, before she saw Mrs. Bryant, back towards her, tending one of the rows of plants. From here she seemed bent and much older than her years. There was no other sign of life from the house.

A stone rolled down the track, but still she did not stir, so, as Carrie reached the softer surface of the lawn, she called softly, "Mrs. Bryant!"

The other woman turned sharply, the small fork slipping from the fingers.

"Carrie!" She put a hand over her mouth, her eyes shocked. "Where have you come from? We . . . thought you were drowned . . . we thought we would never see you again . . ."

"I know, I know . . . oh, I can't tell you how sorry I am," and she ran into those comforting arms outstretched towards her.

After a few moments they drew apart, both a little tearful. "I don't know where Donald is," Mrs. Bryant said, dabbing at her cheeks with a handkerchief.

"He's been beside himself, with all the police out and with every boat in radio contact told to look out for you. You did take the boat, didn't you?"

Carrie nodded. "Yes, and I'm afraid it's gone, somewhere at the bottom of the Indian Ocean. Oh, I know I shouldn't have behaved so stupidly, but I did . . .".

"You're here, safe and sound, that's all that matters. And Donald—how I long to see his face when he sees you're back. I wonder if there's anywhere I can reach him."

"I'm not so sure he'll be so pleased when he knows where I've been."

"What do you mean, Carrie?"

"Mrs. Bryant . . ." Carrie paused, seeking the right words, "I want to ask you something—why is it Donald feels so strongly about Jonas Brandon? I feel at the moment it could come between us."

"I suppose you're telling me that since yesterday you've been on Tern Island?" Mrs. Bryant said with remarkable intuition. "Is that right?"

Carrie nodded. "If Tern Island hadn't been there I really would have drowned. But Jonas did try to tell me that *you* don't feel so strongly against him. Is that true?"

"It's true that I find him a difficult young man, but I certainly don't hold any grudges against him. But my husband and Donald . . . they think rather differently. I wish they didn't, because Mr. Brandon is merely doing what he thinks is right for Mahé and the Seychelles and perhaps for himself. He won't sell us this land, Cinnamon Hill, because he doesn't think the farm will succeed, and he won't let Donald build his marina at the Casuarina Hotel because he thinks it will spoil the coastline. Donald is convinced he has something personal against all Bryants. I've never found that, but . . . well, perhaps Donald

66

hasn't told me everything. As I expect you know, he's a very stubborn young man . . ." she smiled rather wryly, "but then my husband is stubborn too, so perhaps we should just say they're being very masculine." She suddenly seemed to realise that Carrie wore no shoes, and that she was still wearing a bikini and shirt, along with the old khaki hat. "Oh, my dear," she added, "here am I gossiping in the sun, when you'll want to come in and change, and have some lunch. . . ."

"I've had lunch," Carrie assured her with a smile, "but I would like to change. Oh!" she stopped, hearing the sound of wheels on the drive. "Here's Donald, Mrs. Bryant, I think I'd better see him first and at least try to explain."

"Then I'll go in and tell my husband, and we'll see you inside in a few minutes. Oh, I can't tell you how grateful I am that you've been spared. This sea is so kind much of the time, but it can be treacherous for the unwary . . . so treacherous." And she hurried indoors, as if she were about to be overcome by emotion again.

Strangely, because Donald was not expecting to see Carrie, he did not see her. He drove up to park the car, got out, and stood for a moment, as if not knowing quite which way to turn. And then finally, as if realising he was being watched, he turned and saw her, a small slight figure, looking faintly ludicrous in the blue shirt that was too big for her.

In that first tense moment, when he obviously could not believe what he saw, she noticed that his expression changed from one of utter defeat to another of intense joy. His arms were spread towards her, dropping whatever he had in his hand, as he ran and scooped her up as if she were a mere featherweight.

"Carrie, my God, Carrie, have you any idea what

67

we've all been thinking?"

"Yes," she said in a muffled voice, pressed tightly against him. "Yes, I think I have."

"I can't believe it! I really can't believe it. When we saw the boat was gone we didn't think there was a chance in a million that you'd found your way to somewhere safe in all that rain yesterday. Everyone kept telling me not to give up hope, but I think I was *afraid* to hope. . . . Oh, Carrie darling, why did you rush off like that?" When she did not answer for a moment he said, "Was it because of what we said to each other? I didn't mean any of it, really I didn't, but sometimes I speak before I think. I can't help it. But I do trust you, darling, you should know that?"

"How can I know it? she said helplessly. "We're discovering how little we do know about each other. Oh, it doesn't matter; discovery is all part of loving, I suppose, but we must learn not to jump to hasty conclusions. Anyway, Donald," she pulled away from him, and her eyes were very soft and green, "it's I who should apologise, as I said to your mother, Not only have I caused everyone all that worry, but I've smashed up your boat as well. I simply acted without thinking, and I've learned my lesson the hard way."

"Well, all I care about is that you're back." He was still holding tightly to her. "I don't think I've ever been quite so afraid in my whole life. Worst of all was the thought that I'd driven you away from here." He smiled down at her, a warm, loving smile. "Come and sit under the trees for a moment. I don't think I can begin work until I've heard all about what happened to you."

His eyes narrowed. "Talking about what happened, where did you get that shirt, and that terrible hat?"

"I borrowed them," she said tersely. "I lost every-

68

thing I had in the boat, which fortunately wasn't much, only a towel and sunglasses and sandals."

"Go on, darling, tell me."

Carrie took a deep breath and launched into her memory of that nightmare trip. As she talked, telling him of how the rain came down and how everything was blotted out so that she did not even know in what direction she was going, it seemed impossible to think that it was only yesterday. Even now it could have been all a dream, except for the shirt and hat.

"And then," she finished in a low voice, "I sort of felt sand between my toes and fingers, and I must have pulled myself up on to the beach before I passed out. We Flemings have a strong instinct for survival," she added with a wry twist to her mouth.

"But where on earth were you?" he demanded. "I suppose you did find out?"

"Oh yes." she paused, then rushed on. "I was on Tern Island."

For a few moments Donald said nothing, but she could see how hard he stuggled to keep control of his tongue and his emotions.

"I see," he said at last, "and I suppose friend Brandon acted as Sir Galahad."

"If you mean that he and his boys carried me away from the beach and into a hut, and that he loaned me this shirt because of sunburn, then yes, he did act that way."

"Then why the hell didn't he bring you straight back here?" Donald burst out.

It was her turn to struggle to keep calm. This was a testing time for her as well as Donald. "Because," she told him, "I didn't come round until it was almost dark, and much more important, he didn't have a boat."

"Didn't have a boat!" he jeered. "And you actually believed that story. A rich man on his desert island and he didn't have a *boat!*"

"He did not have a boat," she repeated as steadily as she could. "As far as I could gather the motor boat is over here being repaired and the pir . . . pir. . . ."

"Pirogue," he said curtly.

"And the pirogue had taken one of his boys who had an infected foot to the doctor. Whatever you may think, Donald, he was telling the truth. I walked round the whole island this morning, looking at the birds, and there was no sign of another boat."

"Well, then surely he's in radio contact with Mahé? On Cousin, I know for a fact, they use a walkie-talkie. Why is he any different?"

"Because," and now her voice was growing tired, "apparently he doesn't want to be in contact. Does the reason matter, Donald? All I know is that at first I was just as upset as you, thinking of your mother and everyone here searching for me. But I could *see* there was nothing he could do except swim the whole wretched four miles. As it was he hailed the first boat that passed this morning." She stood up. "I think, if you don't mind, I'll go and get some clothes on. I've been in this bikini for two days now and I'm tired of it. I've told you the truth, Donald, that's all I can do. But there is one more thing. . . ."

"Yes?" He was looking down at her.

"If someone as unimportant as Jonas Brandon is going to come between us because of a series of unfortunate coincidences, then it's a great pity I ever came to the Seychelles!" And she stalked off into the house.

70

CHAPTER FIVE

Carrie did not allow herself to be cross for long. She and Donald were doing their loving and learning the hard way. She was sorry he and Jonas rubbed each other up the wrong way, mainly because she was the sort of girl who hated people not getting on with each other. The latter part of her growing up left a scar on her mind, that she had never discussed with anyone. Perhaps the time had come to explain to Donald why any kind of fundamental differences between them could only whittle away her hard-won confidence.

And yet, she realised, she had not questioned her love for Donald, only whether it was right for them to marry. It was so difficult to know whether the two things were the same. Even while she was trying to work out the impossible in her mind she fell asleep, the events of the past few days catching up with her at last.

When she awoke and glanced at her watch she realised it was late afternoon. What on earth must the Bryants think of her? But Mrs. Bryant was quick to explain that she had put her head in about an hour ago, and seeing that Carrie was asleep, had left her.

"I don't think you realise, Carrie, what a jolt to the system all this travelling is, and then to have an experience like yours yesterday . . . why, many a man would be in quite a state of shock. Now you look refreshed and that worried look has gone from your eyes." She smiled warmly at the younger girl. "You mustn't take life so seriously, Carrie, there'll be many problems to face before you're my age, and somehow none of them turn out to be quite as big as you expect."

"I wish I could be like that," Carrie said ruefully, "It's just that. . . ." she stopped, wanting to confide in this warm-hearted woman, but as yet a little too shy to unburden herself.

"You'll talk when you feel like it, I know," Jane Bryant's voice was full of concern, "but for the moment what you really need is a cup of tea. I was going to make one for my husband. Go and talk to him on the verandah . . . he wants to hear all about your adventures."

Carrie still did not yet know quite what to make of Oliver Bryant. His gruff manner hid a kindly man, she was sure, and there were many things about him that reminded her of Donald.

"Hear you've been doing a bit of involuntary bird-watching, young woman," he said, when Carrie came to sit beside him on the dilapidated verandah that was filled with plants and looked out over the sea.

"Yes," she nodded. "I'm very ashamed of myself."

"What's done is done," he remarked, looking at her from under his bushy brows. "Main thing is that you're back safely. I hope that fellow treated you well."

"Very well," she assured him, "except that he doesn't exactly live in the lap of luxury there."

Mr. Bryant snorted. "Inverted snobbery I call it. Nothing more than a drop-out. In my day you worked for a living, however much money you had, especially when you were young and healthy."

Carrie opened her mouth, then closed it again, fearing that even the mildest defence of Jonas Brandon might add fuel to the fire.

But she did stiffen when he went on, "Heard he had a shady past. Ran amok in the States sowing his wild oats a bit too liberally. They say it led to some sort of accident, that's why he's hiding away over here. Wouldn't be a bit surprised if the police had something on him."

"Oh, Mr. Bryant, is that quite fair?" Carrie was protesting at last. "Even if he did have some sort of past, perhaps he's regretting it, perhaps he really wants to make good. Certainly he seems to have achieved a lot on that tiny island. You should go over there and see, if you get the chance."

"I also heard he keeps off maurauders with a shotgun!" But this time she saw his eyes glinting with humour, so she allowed herself to smile back.

"I wouldn't know about that," she said, "but I was certainly lucky to land on Tern Island, whoever the inhabitants might have been."

That evening the Raymonds called in with their small son Simon, a sturdy little boy with a wicked smile. They wanted to make sure that Carrie was well and to tell her and Donald that they were holding a barbecue on Saturday up at their small bungalow high up in the mountains under the shadow of the highest peak known as Morne Seychelle.

"Of course we'll come," said Donald. "Apart from anything else I've been wanting to take Carrie up into the mountains, but there hasn't been time yet."

"Good," said Sally promptly. "Old clothes, please," and to Carrie, "I should actually bring a sweater, the temperature can be ten degrees lower up there, although probably you won't notice it as much as we do."

"It sounds marvellous," Carrie said sincerely. "But can I do anything to help, Sally?"

"Silly, you're our guest of honour. No, seriously, thanks very much, I don't think so, there's not much we can do until the cooking starts. But if I think of anything I'll let you know. We're asking about thirty people, so it should be quite a party." Sally paused. "I'll tell you what, Carrie, I'm going to

Victoria tomorrow to do some shopping. I'd love some company—that is if Donald can spare you."

When Carrie saw Donald hesitate she decided to refuse Sally's offer, but then he said, "Of course I can spare her, I'll be working in the morning at least." She wondered if he had imagined the faintest trace of resentment in his voice. It occurred to her that she had been here for four days and had spent very little time with Donald alone.

After supper that night when they wandered down to the sea, to the now empty boathouse, Carrie tried to tell him she did not mind going with Sally. She was just as happy to stay with him and help.

"No," he said roughly, "you came here for a holiday, and I'm going to see that you get it. There are obviously some things you can do to help Mother, others you can't. Most of my work is heavy at the moment because I'm doing all Dad's as well as my own. You can't help us." He touched her cheek lightly. "I wish it were all working out as I'd hoped, but it isn't, and I feel I'm letting you down."

"No," she said into the soft darkness, "you're not letting me down. If you did come with me every day then I'd feel you were letting your parents down, which would be far worse. Besides, I'm used to spending holidays on my own. I can go exploring and do some sketching. Sally said she would tell me a super place to walk where I could find some more birds and which she says is the most unspoilt corner of the island."

"Then I'll take you tomorrow," he insisted, "after lunch in the cooler part of the afternoon, if that's what you really want to do. Or I could borrow a boat and we could go to Cerf Island. . . . I honestly wish I could take the whole day off, but—well, you can see how it is."

"Perfectly," she said, and reached up to meet his

kiss.

Sally's company was lively the following morning, and she seemed to know her way to every little shop in Victoria.

"Shopping," she explained to Carrie, "is our biggest problem. People forget we're a thousand miles from the nearest coast, Kenya, so unless things are to be fearfully expensive we have to wait for the ships to come in, even now. Sometimes there are no potatoes, sometimes no onions, we run out of the most ridiculous things. It's a little easier now frozen food is getting a little more common, but there have been times when we couldn't even get butter. What makes things even more difficult," she added ruefully, "are the few big hotels. They get the best and we have to have what's left." She smiled suddenly. "I sound as if I'm grumbling, don't I? But there are so many compensations here that a few shortages rarely worry me. If only the soil were better then things would be easy." She dived into the dark interior of a Chinese store which, to Carrie's untutored eye, seemed to stock everything in an area the size of a postage stamp, from motor-bikes to curry powder. After a certain amount of bargaining, she emerged triumphant.

"What were you asking for?" said Carrie curiously.

"Palmiste—or what we call here 'millionaire's salad.' It's literally the heart of the palm tree and one of the most delicious things we can get on the island. The owner of that funny shop is known to be an expert at finding them."

From there they went round the back streets to a French grocery shop, then on to an Indian general general store and finally to the market right in the centre of the town, where Sally filled her bag with peppers and onions and breadfruit and an enormous

75

bunch of bananas.

"Couldn't you buy those things from the Bryants?" Carrie asked.

"Oh, yes," Sally answered, as they piled their purchases into the car, "but Mrs. Bryant is too generous. If I said what I wanted half the time she won't take any money from me. So I only ask when I want one of something—not enough for a whole party. Oh, Carrie," she finished soberly, "they're trying so hard, but I think Cinnamon Hill will beat them."

"What do you mean?" Carrie frowned. "I understood they've made fantastic progress since they came here."

"Oh, they have in a way, but for two steps forward they take one back. The trouble is I think they chose the wrong piece of land. I remember Bill saying the same thing to me when they moved in."

"But . . . but they were farmers in Kenya, weren't they?" Carrie protested.

"Oh yes, but this isn't farming, it's market gardening. There's a man called Jonas Brandon . . . of course you've met him, haven't you, on Tern Island. Well, he advised them not to take this particular piece of land, but Mrs. Bryant had set her heart on it."

Loyally, Carrie said, "Perhaps Jonas Brandon—and everyone else for that matter—is going to be proved wrong. After all, he's not a farmer, is he? Birds are his subject."

Sally shot her a puzzled glance, as if recognising something in her tone, yet not knowing quite what it was. "I suppose so, but he does know an awful lot about the Seychelles. We've known him ever since we arrived. Bill calls him my favourite bachelor, because I'm always trying to do some matchmaking. But of course I'm wasting my time. I'd be surprised if Jonas ever married." With a swift, expert movement, she turned the Mini round. "I know, I've had a great idea. I'll take you along the coast to the best cup of coffee on the island. Have you got the time? I know Donald said he would be working this morning."

"I'd love to come," Carrie nodded. "I'm determined to see as much as I possibly can."

It was only after they had driven about three miles, with Sally chattering away, that Carrie realised in what direction they were heading. Even then she could hardly say, 'Stop, I don't want to go to the Casuarina Hotel—anywhere but the Casuarina Hotel!' Perhaps, she thought hopefully, it was another house along the same stretch of coast, but fate would hardly be as kind as that, particularly when Sally had been talking about Jonas Brandon when she had had the idea about coffee. Still, thought Carrie, her spirits rising again, *he* would certainly not be here and it wasn't Margo who seemed to be lurking round every corner.

They turned down the now-familiar bumpy drive and Sally pulled up the car, beckoning Carrie to follow her as she walked through the passageway calling, "Margo, hi, Margo, are you there?"

Margo appeared from the terrace, dark glasses pushed up into her hair.

"Well, well, what a nice surprise, although I would have expected Donald to have brought you, Carrie, not Sally."

"We've been shopping," Sally said, "and I've been boasting about your coffee." She stopped. "Have you two met already?"

"Twice," Carrie said promptly. "I didn't dream we were coming here, or I would have mentioned it." And then to Margo, "And Donald's working this morning, so he couldn't come."

Margo's eyebrows were raised. "Well, who's

kidding who?" And before Carrie could gauge her meaning she had walked back to the terrace, saying, "Come on, Donald, you'd better confess!"

Donald pulled himself out of the chair, looking decidedly sheepish. There was a half empty glass of beer beside him.

"Hello," said Carrie. "I agree with Margo, this *is* a surprise."

She was unable to keep the touch of frost from her voice.

"Mother had some urgent deliveries after all and then Margo phoned for some extra fruit. By then you'd gone, darling."

"It's quite all right," Carrie returned with a stiff little smile. "You don't have to explain." She turned to Margo with as big a smile as she could manage. "Some of that coffee sounds absolutely marvellous."

"Of course." Margo called something into the depths of the kitchen and then without guile said to Carrie. "I was just saying before you arrived that Donald must bring you up to dinner. I like to show my hand to visitors so they can go back to England and tell all their friends that when they come to the Seychelles, they mustn't miss the Casuarina."

It was Sally who broke the small awkward silence by saying firmly, "There'll be no talk of dinners until after the barbecue on Saturday. You are going to come, aren't you, Margo?"

"My fingers are tightly crossed," the other girl said. "I'll have to get dinner going here and should be with you about nine. You won't be eating before then, will you?"

"Not if I know Bill. He'll still be struggling with the charcoal."

Carrie had not looked at Donald since their first cool exchange. Instead, she had watched Margo, whose lazy, fluid movements spoke of a person trained to move with grace, and while Carrie wanted to believe she was a bit of a bitch, something told her that she wasn't. She merely accepted life as it was presented to her.

Donald now moved towards the door. "I must be off," he said. "Thanks for the beer, Margo." There was a plea in his eyes as he said to Carrie, "Would you like to come with me or . . ."

"I think," she said, in that funny little voice, "I'd like some coffee first. And then Sally and I will be going home. Isn't that right, Sally?"

"In about half an hour," Sally said promptly.

When the coffee came Margo said, "And what did you think of Tern Island? I gather you had an enforced stay?"

Carrie nodded. "Yes. Your . . . your brother-in-law was very kind to me, since I wasn't exactly a welcome guest."

"Then you were lucky. He can be distinctly boorish if he wants to. I hope he let you have a swim off the spit."

"I think that's the place he pulled me out of the water. I didn't see until the next day what a beautiful spot it was."

"Only if you like solitude." Margo pushed her glasses down to cover her eyes and smiled a small secret smile.

It was not until they had left the coast road and were crossing to the other side of the island that Sally said, "I'm sorry if I committed a sort of faux pas, but I'm quite sure Donald was only delivering."

"Yes, I'm sure he was."

"I can promise you that everything was over between them ages ago," Sally babbled on. "There was a time that everyone thought she was going to marry Jonas, but that came to nothing either. Because

79

Margo's so incredibly attractive to men people sometimes think the worst of her, but she's an absolutely super person. She simply can't help looking like she does, and she never lifts a finger to encourage any man. She was absolutely dotty about her husband.''

Carrie sat frozen in her seat, listening to Sally, honest outgoing Sally telling what was obviously the truth as she saw it. Undoubtedly she believed she was offering some kind of comfort to Carrie, but all Carrie could think of was the first time she had seen Margo, spoken to her at the garage, that tiny whisper of doubt. It seemed she could have been right after all.

By the time Sally dropped her off at Cinnamon Hill Carrie was quite composed, smiling and murmuring her thanks, so that she could almost see Sally's imperceptible relaxing.

"Make Donald bring you to the barbecue in good time," Sally called after her. "Bill will need help with the fire and Donald's good at that sort of thing."

"All right." Carrie waved and made her way slowly to the house.

In her room she stood for a moment looking into the mirror, seeing only an ordinary face with too many freckles and hair that though it had undergone subtle changes, had earned her the nickname of 'Carrots' at school. She thought of Margo's easy unconscious beauty and wondered how on earth she could compete with that. It wasn't that she did not like Margo, or even that she was jealous of her—one might as well be jealous of a distant Raquel Welch —it was simply a feeling of hopelessness that this afternoon's incident had engendered. It had taken her all this time to gain enough confidence to fall in love, yet with a single stroke it had all been knocked away.

Carrie tried to tell herself that Donald had come all the way to England, chosen her and practically forced her to return here with him. But could that just have been on the rebound? She would never know. Worse still was the thought that if she did marry Donald it would mean living here on Mahé, seeing Margo . . . probably seeing a lot of her, and always wondering if Donald had any regrets.

Well, she could not sit here all day, wondering about an uncertain future. Most of all she must not let Donald think she had any doubts. It would not do for the two of them to show jealousy. And then, with her hand on the door, a smile on her face, ready to go and join the family for lunch, something else occurred to her. Sally had mentioned that there had also been speculation about Margo and Jonas. Could this be yet another reason for Donald's obsession about the other man? It made as much sense as the business over land and boats.

There were voices outside, so she went and asked Mrs. Bryant if she could help.

"No, dear, thank you very much. Ginette has everything in hand." The older woman was standing in the middle of the room, a faraway expression on her face.

"Is . . . is there something wrong?" Carrie asked.

"To be honest, yes. Some of my precious new seedlings have died. That means there'll be no melons and no onions. It's quite a blow when we'd set so much land aside for them." She turned to her husband sitting with his legs propped up on a stool, his head in a catalogue. "Perhaps, Oliver, we've done the wrong thing over that back strip. Perhaps the soil is worse there."

"Rubbish," he said gruffly, "it's just bad luck. We've been feeding in compost for the past six months. Why should it happen now?"

"I don't know," his wife said helplessly, "but there's another thing. I don't like the look of the new orange trees."

"What's wrong with them?" That was Donald who had just come into the room.

"There are signs of black spot on the leaves. Not serious at the moment, but my instinct tells me that they're not quite right."

"Your instinct, Jane, will lead you into thinking the worst sometimes. The trouble is you worry too much."

She tried to smile. "Sometimes it's difficult not to worry when you see so much work going to waste."

"As soon as I'm up on my feet again," Oliver Bryant said, trying to comfort her, "things will go right. I've a feeling in my bones. And I forgot to tell you, the doctor said the plaster should come off in another two weeks. At least then I'll be able to get about and do something."

Carrie listened to the conversation, selfishly glad that it was on such a general topic whose concern they could all feel. No one asked her how she spent the morning, so she plunged in with more questions about the future plans of Cinnamon Hill, adding, "Was there really any cinnamon here? Is that how it got its name?"

They all laughed and it seemed to lower the tension.

"Cinnamon?" echoed Oliver Bryant. "This island's whole economy is practically based on cinnamon, or at least it was until about five years ago."

"Then what does it look like?" Carrie protested. "I've only seen it ground up in little pots at home. I suppose I've never really thought about it."

Now even Donald was smiling. "I'll show you some afterwards, Carrie. We take it so much for granted, it grows wild all over the island."

"It came from Ceylon originally," Mr. Bryant carried on with the story, "brought here about two hundred years ago. The climate is just right for it and it's never needed to be cultivated. The Indian mynah birds carry the seeds up on to the hillsides and then feed on the berries later. Whoever owns the land on which the cinnamon grows has the right to process and sell it. And just to bore you with one more piece of history—they say it was the search for cinnamon that forced the Portuguese to look for a route round the Cape somewhere in the fifteenth century." He grinned suddenly, looking surprisingly like his son. "And next time I've got a captive audience I'll tell you all about vanilla—*that* has an even stranger history on these islands."

"Another day, Dad." Donald drained his coffee cup, but spoke with humour. "I'm taking Carrie out for a couple of hours."

"But I really would like to hear, Mr. Bryant," Carrie said truthfully. "Somehow growing things like vanilla and cinnamon seems rather exotic."

Outside on the verandah Donald said, "Still want to walk?"

"Please," said Carrie. "I'll go and get my sketch pad."

"And your swimming things," he called after her, "there's bound to be somewhere we can stop."

When they were both in the car he pulled out a map. "Now, where do you want to go?"

She traced the area Sally had suggested to her. "It's here, I think. Sally said I would see some interesting birds."

"And not much else, I thould think. Beyond Port Launay, there's hardly even a road."

"We're going to walk, aren't we," she teased, "so we don't need a road."

"Carrie," he said suddenly, "about this morn-
83

ing. I just want to explain . . . ."

Carrie was very still. "There's nothing to explain, Donald, really there isn't. I'd rather we just left it. It was silly of me to get even mildly huffy. Remember what we said earlier—you trust me and I'll trust you."

"I've known Margo ever since we lived here."

"I know, and I like her too . . . come on, let's go, or the afternoon will have disappeared."

This time they took a completely new route, right over the highest road on the island, climbing and winding through thick trees until suddenly they were among the rolling peaks and looking over green-clad hillsides.

"Tea," Donald told her, "all that you can see from here is tea. If I get a chance I'll arrange a trip for you over the tea factory. It's quite interesting, I believe."

"You mean you've never been?" she mocked him.

"I'm like a Londoner who's never visited the Tower of London."

A little further on he stopped so that she could see from this summit the west coast of the island stretching away far below her. From here, the line of coral was clearly visible, making a ragged barrier between the shore and the deeper turquoise sea beyond.

"Oh, it's beautiful," Carrie breathed. "I know I keep on saying that, and I expect I'll go on saying it, but it's true."

"Yes, it's true," he agreed. "Just a bit too quiet for me sometimes, perhaps."

"But you wouldn't like it all ruined by rows of hotels, would you?" she retorted.

"Of course not, but I don't think you could ever ruin an island like this. Besides, we probably need a few more hotels, they're very thin on the ground, you know."

They met the other coast about ten minutes later and after a few miles the tarmac road petered out to become a hard, red dusty surface.

"There," cried Carrie after a few moments, "you could leave the car under the trees over there."

Donald pulled a face. "You're still set on walking."

"Absolutely," and she held out her hand to him. "It's quite cool under the trees, really it is."

"If you wanted exercise we could swim," he said hopefully.

But already Carrie was walking on ahead, feeling the faint breeze off the sea, lift her hair from her face, and with the freshness of the afternoon her morning's doubts were brushed away.

The track wandered lazily along the coast, dipping and curving first through a glade of casuarina trees, then through a steep cut in the granite rocks.

Carrie recognised the fairy terns swooping high above her, but Donald had to identify the tiny crimson birds that darted in and out of the tall grasses and the mangroves. She sat down on a boulder and pulled out her notebook, drawing in swift sure strokes, while Donald lay back in the sun, hoping she had travelled far enough on foot.

For the last half hour they had not seen a single human being, but suddenly from round the next bend came a man walking slowly, with something on his head.

Carrie stared at this strange sight, for a moment not recognising his burden.

"What is it, Donald?"

"A turtle," he said laconically.

She stared again and realised the creature was upside down, his head and tail twisting feebly.

"But it's alive," she said, shocked. "What's he

going to do with it?"

"Kill it eventually. To one of the poorer islanders it's the most valuable thing he can catch. There's steak and soups from the flesh and all the souvenirs in the shops from the shell."

The man had stopped and was talking to Donald in the queer mixture of English and French tongues that made up the Creole language.

"But it's cruel," she cried. "Please, Donald, can't you ask him to put it back in the sea?" Even as she spoke it seemed to her that the turtle was heaving great mournful sighs and from its eyes were dropping bitter tears. It was too much for Carrie.

"Put that down!" she cried sharply.

As the man stared at her in amazement, Donald said, "Don't be daft, Carrie, turtles always make that noise, and if he puts it down out of the water the wretched creature will suffocate."

"Ask him how much he wants for it," she demanded.

"I know without asking that it will be more than you or I can afford. What this man gets will probably keep his family for weeks."

"I don't care what it costs," she said fiercely, "that turtle has got to go back into the sea. Are you going to tell him, Donald, or am I? And she stood there, legs apart, hands on her hips waiting for his answer.

CHAPTER SIX

It seemed to Carrie that she stood there for ever, with Donald staring at her in utter disbelief. Then he came across, put his hands on her shoulders and shook her slightly.

"Carrie, this isn't a man, or a child—this is a *turtle*."

"I'm perfectly well aware of what it is, but I will not see it suffering like that!"

Without warning his surprise turned to anger. "Then I suppose you'd save every pig, every chicken —every fish that's caught! Grow up, Carrie, these people have to have a living just as fishermen and farmers do. You can't change the world."

The man had walked away, and as Carrie watched him go her shoulders slumped and she started to cry. If someone had asked her she could not really have told why she cried, only that she could not have stopped herself if she had tried.

"Carrie, Carrie darling . . . you're overwrought, suffering from delayed shock after your experience at Tern Island. Here, sit down, have a rest and we'll go back to the car, or swim if you like."

She let him dry her eyes and the comfort of his arms about her helped a little. Was she really crying for a doomed turtle, or was he right? Her brush with death could possibly have left its mark, and yet the cause of her distress seemed to go deeper than that.

She sniffed at last and tried to smile. "I'm sorry, Donald, nothing seems to be going quite right. Perhaps it would have been better if you'd never asked me to come."

"Don't say that, Carrie, please; it's only the

thought of you coming over here has kept me going
for the past few weeks. I'm not a farmer, I don't even
like it particularly, but I'm sort of trapped until
Dad gets better. It's not just you who feel things are
going wrong, but the whole of Cinnamon Hill has
hit a bad streak."

"Donald?"

"Yes, darling?"

"Do you honestly think your parents can make a
success of it?"

"I don't know. At the moment things don't look
so good. I sometimes wish they'd never got the place.
Now perhaps you can begin to see that if the land
was theirs at least they could sell it and recount their
losses if all else failed."

She lifted her head. "And what could the land be
used for?"

"Why, it's the most perfect site for a hotel."

This one Carrie could not answer. Donald wanted more hotels, Jonas Brandon wanted none. Who
was right? She had not the least idea, except that the
thought of monster buildings all over this beautiful
island appalled her. Hotels meant cars and cars
meant wider roads. She looked up and down the one
they were on. Not a single car had passed while
they had been walking.

Donald stood up and gave her his hand. Slowly
she allowed herself to be pulled up beside him. He
kissed her firmly. "I've decided we'll swim. At least
it will cool us and something will be salvaged from
the wreckage of the afternoon. I noticed a tiny cove,
not far from where we parked the car."

So they went and got their swimming things and
climbed down over the rocks to the crescent-shaped
beach that was strewn with old coconut shells and
fringed by palm and takamaka trees. This time
there was no sand underfoot when they walked into

88

the water, only sharp stones, so they climbed round the smooth granite boulders at the edges of the cove into the deeper pools that swirled and eddied round the rocks. Although it was different it had its own kind of enchantment, for Carrie caught sight of her first baby octopus in the shallower pools and saw the fish leaping like swift flashes of silver above the water.

When they came out at last Donald called her over. "Come and look, Carrie, a real cinnamon tree. You can actually see for yourself."

She watched, fascinated, while he stripped off a piece of young bark and rolled it in his fingers until it became a sort of quill.

"There," he said, "when it's dried it curls right up and a dozen or so of these little sticks go to make up the packets you can buy at any of the tourist shops."

Carrie sniffed. "It doesn't actually smell like cinnamon, does it?"

"It will," he grinned, "don't worry, it will."

As they lay against one of the smooth rocks, drying out, Carrie said lazily, "Donald, you haven't really told me what you're going to do when your father's well again and you can start on your own. Oh, I know we talked about it a bit in England, but somehow it was all so remote then that I couldn't imagine how you were going to operate as a travel agent here—and I'm not sure that I do even now. I mean, would you take people to Kenya, or even England?"

"Good lord, no—at least I suppose that would be a far-off dream. I would operate strictly within the Seychelles. With the expanding tourist business here there's room for specialist travel people. I've got a friend who works for a big agent in Kenya, who knows these islands well and is an expert on hotels and all that side. I want to concentrate all the local excursions that actually use the water. We would start off with a couple of boats and take people to the obvious places like La Digue and Praslin and some of the smaller islands. Then we would run snorkelling trips and go out deep sea fishing and charter the boats for the day, perhaps. Eventually I would want to take people to the Amirantees."

"Where's that?" Carrie asked curiously.

"Oh, it's all part of the Seychelles group, but about a hundred and fifty miles away. The islands are virtually uninhabited except for the birds, but there's simply fantastic fishing round all the coral reefs and I believe the skin-diving is good too. I've never been yet, but it's the first thing I'll do when I get a week's holiday. That's all just the beginning, Carrie," he went on eagerly, "because after that there are all the sailing boats we could hire out, and of course the glass-bottomed boats over the reef." He reached for her hand. "What do *you* think of it, darling? After all, it's going to be your life as much as mine."

"It sounds very exciting, but," she added ruefully, "I hope I would be useful. At the moment I don't suppose you'd let me near another boat."

He squeezed her hand. "It wasn't the boat—it was simply because you didn't know enough about the Seychelles and its weather. But, talking about boats, a lot depends on us finding somewhere to use as a temporary marina. The Casuarina would be perfect, absolutely perfect, as a jumping-off point for the trips, and I think Margo would even let us rent a room as an out-of-town office."

Trying not to sound in any way carping, Carrie said lightly, "Margo seems very interested in the whole project. Does she know a lot about travel and boats, too?"

"Yes, she does. Her husband used to run away with most of the big fishing contests round here." He paused as though he were choosing his next words carefully, "She . . . she's offered to help George and myself raise some of the money we need, or at least offer her harbour free."

"And what would she expect in return for that?" Carrie asked before she could stop herself.

"A small share in the business," Donald said shortly. He sat up, and although she had her eyes tightly closed, she knew he was looking down at her. "Carrie, please don't imagine things that aren't there. I've known Margo—ever since I've been coming to the Seychelles. She's now a business woman and there's nothing more to it than that. I daresay she could have any man on this island merely by flicking her little finger, but she doesn't want that. Ever since Hugh died she's been friendly with a lot of people, but she keeps them all at arm's length."

Carrie opened her eyes and looked directly at him. It was better to get things out into the open.

"And if she flicked her little finger at you?"

Donald did not answer for a moment, but she imagined she saw a tiny muscle move at the corner of the mouth. Then he said flatly, "It was you I asked to marry me, Carrie, you I fell in love with. There's nothing more to my friendship with Margo than there is with, say, Sally, or a dozen other pretty girls on this island. You're seeing things that don't exist."

Carrie sat up and then let her head rest against his bare shoulder. "Then as far as I'm concerned, darling, it's forgotten. But it was still better to *ask* you, rather than go on wondering. I like Margo, I like her very much, although I think I'm a little nervous of her sophistication. I just want us to be open with each other, that's all."

"Carrie," he said from above her head.

"Yes?"

"Are you going to marry me?"

"Ask me again at the end of the three weeks. I promise you," she said softly, "you'll have my answer then."

"If you say 'no', Carrie, I think I'll go out of my mind."

She pulled away from him, hearing the tenseness in his voice, and said half-mockingly, "Why should I say no? It's just my cautious nature coming out. At least your mother and father have passed the test. I think they're both lovely."

"Well, that's something," The schoolboy grin was back on his face. He jumped up and held out his hand. "Come on, Miss Cautious, you've reminded me of where my duty lies. It's home to work or Cinnamon Hill will never get on its feet!"

It was the night of the Raymonds' barbecue. Although there had been a typical Mahé shower during the late afternoon, the sun had come out again to dry the ground and now the air was cool and fresh.

Carrie had been helping in the garden for most of the day, but now she had showered and changed into her favourite white trousers and an emerald green silky cotton shirt and brushed her tawny hair until it gleamed. Peering into the mirror for a final check, she was relieved to see that her English whiteness had gone and her skin had already taken on a warmer tone. Not exactly tanned yet, but definitely warmer.

She came out on to the verandah where the two older Bryants were having their coffee. Both looked at her, then Mr. Bryant said gruffly, "Wish I were twenty years younger, Carrie, then I can tell you Donald wouldn't stand a chance."

His wife laughed, her brown eyes twinkling. "He was quite a one for the girls, Carrie, I used to have to watch my laurels. Perhaps it's just as well he *is* laid up with that leg." She stood back and smiled. "But he's quite right, Carrie, you look really charming."

Impulsively, Carrie hugged the older woman. "Thank you," she said softly, "and thank you for making me so welcome at Cinnamon Hill. I love it here, I really do."

"And we love having you, dear, I only hope . . ." she stopped. "But I mustn't try to influence you . . . you're here to make up your own mind, aren't you?"

Carrie nodded.

From outside Donald roared, "Are you coming, Carrie? We're going to be the last there and all the grub will be gone!"

"Coming!" She grabbed her bag and fled down the old steps.

As she got in the car, he kissed her soundly. "You look good enough to eat—and I'm famished."

"You don't look so bad yourself," she teased him. In fact he looked very handsome, with his thick fair hair brushed, wearing a dark brown shirt and cream-coloured slacks. She was proud to be with him.

As they drove up into the mountains the air grew noticeably cooler. It was the first time. Carrie realised, that she had been up above the coast in the dark. Looking back, as Donald manoeuvred the hair-pin bends she could see the lights winking far below, and out in the harbour a large ship was at anchor, even more brightly lit.

Carrie felt happy and relaxed. "I'm looking forward to this evening," she said. "It sounds just the sort of informal do I adore. And the Raymonds are so nice and friendly, they must know some nice people."

"They do," he said. "We're lucky to have them as neighbours. And this place up here they more or less built themselves, just so that Sally and little Simon can escape some of the worst of the weather when it's really stinking hot and humid.''

A few minutes later he turned off the road and drove along a rough track from where Carrie could hear the sound of music and laughter.

"Welcome," called Sally, as they piled out. "Everybody, this is Carrie Fleming from England ... Donald, you'll have to do the honours, as the food is in a critical state. Help yourself to red or white wine or beer ... they're all on the table over there."

Carrie found herself shaking a dozen hands and she hardly remembered a single name, but everyone was eager for news of home, and the few French who were there wanted to know about the political situation. Like everywhere else on Mahé, Carrie found there was a mixture of colours and languages, much of it Creole, which she was just beginning to recognise.

The setting for the little wooden bungalow was perfect, among a clearing of trees of every sort. There was no electricity, but paraffin lamps hung from the roof, and all round the edges of the lawn were candles that had been set in sand in tall brown paper bags, so the whole garden seemed to be aglow with fairy lights.

Somehow she got separated from Donald almost immediately, as someone asked him a question about fishing and she wandered over to the actual barbecue that had been constructed out of a split oil drum filled with charcoal that was already changing from red to white ash, over which was a grill.

"It looks very ingenious," Carrie said to Bill, as he turned sausages and pieces of chicken with a long fork.

"We have to be ingenious up here," he returned. "The whole place is very primitive, just a large wooden hut really that we grace with the name of bungalow. But the garden is beautiful. Simon loves it nearly as much as the beach."

As she sipped her glass of wine, Carrie found herself talking to an oldish man who had lived in the Seychelles for most of his life and who told her what Victoria was like twenty years ago, with all wooden buildings and corrugated roofs, and how when he first came he had stayed at a hotel on the west coast and walked the three miles by bridle path over the hills to the capital. If they were lucky the ships called once a month.

"Now," he said gloomily, "with this airport everything is different."

"Did you like it better then?" she asked.

"To be honest, yes, but then I've always liked the simple life. I know one can't stand in the way of progress, so the airport had to come, but all I'm praying is that the true simplicity which is the joy of these islands will not vanish. But then I'm an old man . . . you young people enjoy fun and entertainment, so I mustn't be selfish."

Carrie was just about to reassure him that not everyone wanted the same kind of holiday island, when his attention was called and she found herself standing alone for the first time.

"Hello, Carrie."

She looked up, startled. "Jonas! I didn't know you were going to be here."

"Neither did I. I came over to bring back the bigger boat and bumped into Sally this morning. She made me promise to come."

There was a moment's awkward silence, then they both started to talk together.

"Go on," said Carrie breathlessly, "please. I was only going to ask you about your boy's foot."

"Nearly healed, thank you very much. I was going to remark on the fact you were talking to old Harry

Driver."

"Yes, he was telling me about the old days of Mahé."

"A man after my own heart—a conservationist. But he's more knowledgeable about this island than almost anyone else. And he loves it, too. It was he who told me that Tern Island was for sale—once he knew I wasn't going to turn it into a tourists' paradise!" He paused. "I presume our American friends got you back safely—and no repercussions."

"No, no repercussions," but her hesitation was just a fraction too long.

"Then we must do something about that," he said quietly.

"I . . . I don't understand." She looked up at him uncertainly, and found him looking at her, his eyes reminding her of the blue-black shimmer of a raven in flight, yet giving nothing away. She had not the least idea why he should be able, merely by looking at her, to make her feel like a gauche schoolgirl.

"I don't like feuds, do you?"

Carrie shook her head.

"Then are you going to ask Donald to bring you to Tern, so you can finish your sketches?"

Suddenly Carrie knew she wanted to do that as much as anything. And he was quite right, feuds were for children or old men. At this moment something told her it was important to heal the breach between Donald and this man who had in some mysterious way changed the pattern of her relationship with Donald.

"I'd like to come," she told him. "I went across the island to that bay you mentioned and although it was very beautiful and I saw some red cardinals, it. . . ."

" . . . had nothing on Tern Island," he finished for her.

She joined with his laughter. "That's right," and

96

then out of the corner of her eye she saw Donald talking to Margo. Now was the time for a confrontation, she thought, the perfect moment. If Donald was going to be difficult, then she in turn could be difficult.

They were standing beside a bush full of sweet-scented pale blue flowers. In her nervousness, Carrie found she was rubbing one of the blooms between her fingers.

"Do you know what it is?" he asked, his long fingers picking out the spray just above her head.

"No."

"It's the yesterday, today and tomorrow tree. See, here's one of yesterday's flowers, already faded, now one of today's still fresh, and there's tomorrow's bud, just ready to open. I think we humans could learn a lot from this tree, always looking forward, ready to start the new day."

She thought she knew what he was trying to say to her, but she could not put her thoughts into words, so she rushed on, "There's Donald . . . over there, talking to your sister-in-law. Why don't we go across and ask him?"

"All right. In fact, that's an excellent idea." But the look he gave her before striding across the lawn had not a little cynicism in it.

"Hello, Margo," she said breathlessly. "Donald . . .".

"Yes?" His voice was distinctly cool as he saw who she was with and her heart sank. Nevertheless she ploughed on relentlessly. "Donald, Mr. Burton has suggested that you take me to Tern Island one day so I can finish my sketches of bird life there. Could we do that, do you think?"

Before Donald could answer—and if he had given an answer then Carrie knew what it would have been—Margo put in lazily, "What a good idea,

Carrie, and if you two don't mind me playing goose-berry, then perhaps we could make a day of it. How about that, brother-in-law?" And she challenged him with her smile.

"Fine. That provides us with a cook as well as an artist."

"Oh, no," she shook her head. "Since I never get asked, I'm actually inviting myself as a visitor. Strictly no chores. They do say," she added sweetly, "you're not such a bad cook yourself."

While this badinage was going on, Carrie was watching Donald's face. Some of the first flash of anger had left it, but he did not look particularly happy at the idea.

"Well, Donald," she said at last, very quietly, "you haven't said yet whether you'll come."

He waited just a moment longer, as if seeking a way out of this unwelcome challenge, but when he saw them all looking at him, he said grudgingly, "If that's what you want, Carrie, then we'll go."

An odd smile tilted the corner of Jonas's mouth, then he said drily, "I think we'd better make this date before you all change your minds. I'll send the boat for you on Sunday."

"We'll come in mine," Donald said quickly, before he remembered he had no boat.

"I'd offer mine," said Margo," but by the time I've come all round the north of Mahé, Jonas will be there and back. I'll drive across to Cinnamon Hill and you can pick us up from there, Jonas. I presume we're invited to lunch."

"I shall consult with my chef tomorrow." Jonas gave her an ironic bow. "And now I think we're being called to eat tonight's meal. Stock up, Carrie . . . remember we live simply."

"If that delicious fish means simple living," she retorted, "then I'm all for it."

Donald steered her away and towards the barbecue. "How on earth did you get us landed with that?" he hissed.

"I didn't," she said calmly. "He asked me, and I had no alternative. After all, if it hadn't been for him. . . ."

"I know, I know," he said crossly, "but I presume you've thanked him, you can't go on being grateful for the rest of your life."

Carrie turned on him. "I'm going to see the birds, Donald," she said tightly, "*not* Jonas Brandon."

"Maybe, but the fellow's cropping up just a little to often for my liking."

They were standing a little way away from the other guests and Donald had her by the hand. Carrie, determined not to get cross tonight, cocked her head on one side, saying, "Every time he 'crops up' as you put it, it's been an accident. I have another fortnight here, so if the law of averages is right, then I daresay he'll crop up again. We can't let him come between us, like like some sort of bad dream. What happens if I come to live here, Donald? I won't be able to avoid him then, just as you can't avoid Margo.'

"That's different!"

"Not really," she said, "at least, not to me. I'm famished. Come on, those sausages are smelling absolutely gorgeous," and she pulled him over to join the others.

The whole evening, even with that awkward moment, was wonderful. There were sausages and hamburgers, chicken and breadfruit chips, with mounds of salad and home-made rolls, all tasting deliciously of charcoal. Afterwards someone got out a guitar and a small group of the guests sang Creole songs. There was plenty of wine and it did not take Donald long to forget that brief embarrassment with Jonas Brandon. Carrie could not help noticing that Jonas

99

moved easily amongst all the guests, apparently knowing most of them, but spending more time than any with the old islander who knew so much Seychellois history. If he were friendly with these people, and if he was so close to the Raymonds who were obviously one of the most popular couples on the island, then his reputation as a 'rich layabout' must be exaggerated. One day when she and Sally were alone together, perhaps she could probe a little more deeply, for she was still curious to know why any man should cut himself off from the world, and also what the accident was that he had so briefly mentioned.

Donald and she drove down the mountainside well after midnight, pausing to watch the moon over the far horizon, throwing its path of silver across the dark water.

He put his arm round her and kissed her and she responded with all her heart, trying to show him that for her love was truly only a couple of weeks away. And yet, she decided, love must show itself in so many mysterious ways, for tonight, although she stayed in his arms for a long time, there was no leap of the blood, no fire that she had always associated with the heady feeling of being in love. Perhaps, she thought, with just a tinge of doubt, the 'grand passion' was not for her after all.

CHAPTER SEVEN

The next few days fell into a kind of smooth easy pattern and Carrie began to feel that she had been in the Seychelles for ever. England, those thousands of miles away, seemed like another planet, and the thought of going back filled her with a quiet desperation. To wake up each morning to feel the sun, to look out and see the palms bending gracefully towards the sparkling sea, was like catching a glimpse of paradise.

Gradually she was managing to find jobs she could do at Cinnamon Hill, without showing too much ignorance. She took over the evening watering and much of the morning deliveries, leaving Donald and his mother to concentrate on the animals and the actual growing. Fortunately, after that first time, Donald had raised no more objections about her visiting the Casuarina Hotel and so it had become part of her morning pattern to drop in for coffee with Margo.

One morning, as they sat on the terrace, with the sun blazing down and the temperature well into the eighties, Margo squinted up at the cloudless sky and said, "We're going to be in trouble if we don't have rain soon."

"Rain?" exclaimed Carrie, aghast. "You don't mean the kind of rain that fell that awful day I was in the boat?"

Margo laughed. "Well, not quite like that, and preferably at night, but normally at this time of year the rainfall should be much higher. As far as I can remember we've only had the odd shower since you arrived."

"One, I think," Carrie agreed.

"Well, the first thing that happens is a chronic water shortage—and that's no fun, I can tell you, especially in a hotel. The loos don't work and we have to ration baths. But the people who will really suffer are those like the Bryants."

"I know," said Carrie soberly. "Mrs. Bryant was saying only yesterday that the whole pepper crop looks like failing . . . and there are others on the danger list. She's beginning to look worried, and, Margo, she does work so hard, and all through the heat."

"Well," said Margo practically, "the islands are going through a time of change. In the past the ordinary Seychellois people were content to live on rice and fish and fruit in season. Work and money were not too important so long as they were happy. But now the big hotels have come and are offering what seems like high wages, so lots of them are leaving the land, which after all is extremely hard work for very little reward. Oh, I think things will change again, but whether it's in time to help people like the Bryants, I don't know. Jonas says. . . ." she stopped abruptly.

"What does Jonas say?" Carrie insisted.

"Oh, nothing really." Margo stood up and leaned over the terrace to stare down into the still blue water below. "I suppose I've learned to cope with Jonas's whims. Donald hasn't, so it's best not to talk about it if I want to stay friendly with both men. And I do." She turned her huge expressive eyes upon Carrie.

There was suddenly no time like the present, so Carrie came across and joined her, to sit on the edge of the little wall. "Tell me, Margo," she said, "why has Jonas sort of opted out?"

Margo eyed the younger girl speculatively. "Normally, I wouldn't say anything, as Jonas loathes talking about his past, but I think you're the first girl for a long time he's actually spoken of without cynicism."

Carrie blinked. "But I hardly know him."

"Maybe, but he said the other day that you have two qualities he admires, guts and serenity. So at least I'm prepared to tell you something, even if it's only to make you understand him a bit when Donald explodes."

"Go on." Carrie encouraged, as the other girl's long fingers moved restlessly over the smooth granite.

"I'm only going to tell you about the accident, because I feel it's that which had most effect on his life. You see, a few years back Jonas was a racing driver, one of the top few on the American circuit. People said he might have been world champion one day. He had a great friend called Alan who was also a driver . . . I believe the two of them were known as the Terrible Twins. They used to drive for the same owner. Anyway, one day they joined forces to enter a big rally to raise money for charity. They were odds-on favourite to win in their car. I'm not entirely sure quite what happened except that I think Jonas, who was actually at the wheel, hit a bad patch of grease and the car went out of control. They crashed and it was some time before anyone found them. Alan was much the most badly hurt of the two, but Jonas was conscious and couldn't pull his friend out of the wreckage."

Margo paused, as if the memory of this accident was too much, and Carrie was about to tell her not to go on, but then she seemed to take a grip of herself and finished in a tight, hard voice, "They were both in hospital together. I don't honestly know whether Alan would have lived anyway, his injuries were rather bad and in particular his face was smashed up

103

and so were both his legs, but what Jonas remembers as the worst was that Alan's wife more or less gave him up for dead, and hardly came to see him in hospital, either from acute distress or—Jonas believes—from revulsion. At any rate, because of her . . . her defection, Alan simply gave up the will to struggle. Jonas believes himself responsible for his friend's death . . . though dozens of people have assured him the same could have happened to anyone, and it's given him a real thing about women." She added with a wry twist to her mouth. "He's convinced that they're all right for 'playthings', but nothing more. That's why I don't think he'll ever marry; the hurt over Alan and his wife went so deep that he simply can't forget. Before the accident he was known to be a real lad about town, a bit wild, anything for a bit of adventure. Now, it's as if there's only the shell left. The only thing I can say that living over on Tern, engrossed in the work he's doing there, some of the surface wounds are healing. Now he mixes with people he knows and likes. There was a time, Carrie, when he could hardly be persuaded to come to Mahé at all. At least that has changed."

There was something in Margo's voice that made Carrie turn quickly and look at her. And she discovered that a lost look in the eyes almost matched that voice.

"*You* seem to understand Jonas," Carrie pointed out.

"I've known him a long time." Margo shrugged.

"Have . . . have you ever thought of marrying him?" Carrie knew she had no right to ask such a question of this girl she had only known a week, but had she wanted to she could not have held back the impulse.

Margo threw her head back and laughed.

"Oh, I'm sorry." Carrie was contrite. "I should

never have said that, but I just hate to see people un-happy."

"I don't mind. At least you've said what a lot of other people have thought. No," Margo shook her beautiful head, "although Jonas and I are close in many ways, and we'd probably stick up for each other ... shoulder to shoulder and all that ... in most others it would be like mixing sand and water. We have respect and disapproval for each other in about equal quantities. And *that's* no basis for a marriage. Besides," she added flatly, "I don't love him."

Carrie stood up, "I think," she said hastily, "it's time I went. I promised Donald I'd have the van back by midday. I ... I'm sorry to get so personal, Margo, I didn't set out to ask all those questions, they just sort of ... came out."

"Yes, I know. I'm inquisitive too. But since you've asked me questions, perhaps I can ask you one?"

"Of course." Carrie stopped in the doorway.

"You're probably going to marry Donald, aren't you?"

"Probably." It was Carrie's turn to be cautious.

"I think in the end I may persuade Jonas to let me use this little harbour commercially. Oh, I don't mean fill it with hundreds of boats, and run a sort of club here—just an anchorage for half a dozen boats."

Carrie watched, knowing something else must be coming.

"I was just wondering," Margo went on with an air of apparent carelessness, "if you would really mind if Donald and I had a partnership over his business. I think it's the only way he'll ever get going."

Carrie lifted her chin. "Why should I mind? He's told me all about it."

"Maybe, but when you called unexpectedly the other day, and found him here, I had the distinct feeling you jumped to all the wrong conclusions."

Uncomfortably, Carrie moved back on to the terrace, "I suppose you're right," she admitted honestly, "but it was only because I didn't know you then. After Donald told me about his plans—well, then it all seemed different. I suppose we know so little about each other."

"*Do* you love him, Carrie?"

In the end Carrie never had to answer that question, because one of the hotel staff came rushing out for Margo to solve some domestic emergency, and Carrie took this as her cue to be on her way back to Cinnamon Hill.

About half way through Sunday morning Margo drove across the island, and soon after she had arrived Carrie and Donald watched a beaming Johnny draw carefully into the small landing stage by the empty boathouse. They took with them only swimming things and a sketch pad for Carrie, for Donald had said emphatically that he had to be back well before dark to feed the livestock.

As they waited Carrie put a small hand in his and said, "If you really don't want to go, Donald, I shan't mind. It was difficult to say no up at the barbecue. We could make some excuse when Margo comes...."

"No." He shook his head. "We'll go, we said we would. We can hardly leave Margo to go on her own."

Tern Island looked almost more picturesque today, with its spit of sand catching the sun and glinting like molten gold and the deeper water inside the reef changing from turquoise to emerald. It was just like a storybook idea of a desert island.

There was, Carrie saw this time, quite a broad passage across the reef, so that she need never have hit bottom had she kept her wits about her that day.

Jonas and one of the other boys were waiting for their arrival, to haul in the boat as the tide carried them on to the sand.

Jonas gave his sister-in-law a peck on the cheek and greeted Donald and Carrie courteously, asking them to make themselves at home. He poured them drinks of fresh lime, then suggested they swim before lunch. Carrie was only too glad to persuade Donald into the water, for he was already looking ill at ease as if he half regretted coming after all.

As they lay on the warm sand afterwards, Donald said, "I don't know how he can live here. There's nothing absolutely nothing—except this patch of beach and the water here."

"And the birds," Carrie reminded him.

Donald sat up and rubbed his hair with a towel. "Oh, sure, the birds—*if* you like only birds for company. I think I'd go off my nut if I stayed here more than a day."

"Funny," said Carrie lazily, "I thought it was a sort of enchanted island."

He snorted. "Take off your rose-coloured spectacles and you'll see there's no water, so therefore practically no vegetation—only casuarina trees and some scrub—and even that looks as if it's having a struggle to grow."

Carrie looked about her and supposed he was probably right. But she had not seen Tern Island quite like that, only as a small but truly unique haven of peace. As she squinted up into the sky high above her she saw the huge black angular wings of a frigate bird as it seemed to circle the island like a guard on duty.

"You don't mind," she said, "if I really do spend a half an hour after lunch doing some sketching? That's what we really came for, isn't it?"

He shrugged. "It's O.K. by me. I'll go and find

107

the tortoises. I've been in the Seychelles all this time and never seen a giant tortoise, so my afternoon won't be wasted either." He touched her cheek, seeing her anxious expression. "Don't worry, Carrie, I'll mind my manners. After all, I am a guest, aren't I?"

In fact, Carrie noticed with relief, the little lunch party went off quite well. Jonas plied them with white wine that he had mysteriously managed to keep quite cool and served an excellent lunch which, he explained to Carrie, was done as near the Creole way as was possible on his primitive stove.

There was *tec-tec* soup to start with, which was something like a clear broth with dozens of tiny 'cockles' in it, caught, Margo told her, on the sandy shore as the tide recedes. After that there was a choice of octopus cooked in coconut milk and some curried lobster with green mango salad and fried bananas.

"I must say," said Margo, sipping at her cup of black coffee, "you don't do so badly after all, Jonas. And here am I feeling so sorry for you that I go to great pains to give you a square meal when you come over."

Jonas eyed her thoughtfully. "This is my one party menu, didn't you know? Carrie will confirm that my usual diet is grilled fish, or grilled fish."

"That's right." But Carrie was looking at Margo, not Jonas, who in spite of having swum earlier managed to look as if she had stepped straight from a modelling assignment, her black glossy hair pulled up to make a knot on top of her head, her tanned body without an ounce of spare flesh only just covered in the smallest of scarlet bikinis. How could Jonas possibly not fall in love with her?

When Carrie said she was going to take her sketch pad to the other side of the island, Margo yawned and said she supposed that Jonas was going to work and she would show Donald the tortoises before she had an afternoon nap. And so they all went their different ways.

Carrie retraced her steps and found again the little chick nesting in the hollow of the casuarina, in exactly the same position as he had been a week ago, only now he was just a little larger and fluffier. She rubbed a finger along the length of his warm downy feathers and smiled delightedly when he did not move.

For a little while Carrie sat absorbed, her pencil flying over the paper with surer and surer strokes as she tried to capture all that she was seeing. When she moved on it seemed to her that she was alone on the island except for the whirr and movement of the birds high above her. Therefore, when the sound came from somewhere near her feet, she stopped, uncertainly. It was like a faint cheep, and then there was a rustle in the dry undergrowth.

Moving cautiously through the shadowy trees, Carrie was not quite certain what she was looking for, only she remembered Jonas's warning to watch her step for fear of treading on a nest.

Even so, she almost missed the small, olive-coloured bird that lay at her feet. When she bent down to look, it fluttered wildly, but only moved a few inches, and she saw that one wing dragged behind it along the ground.

"Oh, you poor little thing!" Carrie breathed, bending down to meet the small brown frightened eyes. She did not know whether to touch it, lift it up and try to take it to Jonas, or to get Jonas to come here. In the end she decided on the latter course of action, marking the spot with a tall stick and praying that no predator would attack a wounded bird. She ran back on to the path and as she drew near the huts called Jonas's name. It was Johnny who came out to her and, breathlessly, she asked him to fetch his master. Afraid she would not find the place again, she started back, and there Jonas found her, hovering on the edge of the path.

"What's happened?" he said crisply.

"It's one of the birds . . . I think a broken wing," she told him, and led the way back through the crackling undergrowth.

The bird was just where she had left it and when Jonas's big hand cradled it with the gentleness of a child, it did not move, but lay there, with only trust, not fear, in its eyes.

"It's one of your rare brush warblers, isn't it?" Carrie asked.

"You're learning quickly." He shot her a brief smile.

"Can you do anything to help it?"

"Oh, yes." He stood up, examining the useless wing. "I'll take him back to the lab and patch up the wing. A week or so in captivity and he should be free again—and able to fly. But he wouldn't have lasted long on the ground here. Wounded birds don't even if they're not attacked. Do you want to come back and watch?"

"Please," said Carrie.

She stood by silently as he fixed the wing in a tiny splint, then bound it so that it lay quite stiff. Then he put the little bird in one of the empty cages at the end of the lab and carried it out to a shady spot. He poured out cold drinks for both of them and they carried the glasses to the chairs under the trees. "How's the drawing going?"

"Fine—except I've left my sketch pad somewhere over there. I must go and get it. . . ." Carrie half rose in her seat, but his hand on her arm pressed her gently back.

"It's too hot to go racing around the island at this time of day. Johnny will get it for you."

She sat back again, realising she was hot. Idly, she wondered where the others were, but she decided she did not even want to go in search of them.

"I'm keeping you from your work," she said suddenly, aware that Jonas was watching her.

"No. Nothing keeps me from work when I want to work. It's Sunday, isn't it? I can take a couple of hours off. Or are you bored with my company?"

"Oh, no," she said quickly, and realised she spoke the truth. Whatever she might think of this man, she could never be bored with him. "I was thinking that . . . that there was something I wanted to ask you?"

"I can guess what it is." He allowed himself a slight smile, but all the time he watched her. "It's about the Bryants . . . I imagine things are a little rough for them at the moment."

"Then if you know that. . . ."

"I can't make it rain," he reminded her with faint irony.

"Of course not." Now that she had started she could not stop herself. "But if all the crops do fail, they'll have lost everything."

"And that will be my fault?" His thick, dark eyebrows were raised.

"No, at least not in some ways . . . but if you'd allowed them to buy the land. . . ."

"Oh, come, come, Carrie, you're very loyal, if somewhat misguided. I knew the chances of Cinnamon Hill surviving as a nursery garden were slender —whatever faith Mrs. Bryant had in the scheme. To sell them the land would have been tantamount to suggesting they build a hotel in that very spot. And I'll fight that project to the last ditch."

"You're a very hard man," she said quietly.

"But at least I'm true to myself." He stood up abruptly and the old harsh note was back in his voice. "Go and marry your Donald, grow up a little, and stop seeing the world in black and white. If Donald sent you as his messenger. . . ."

"He didn't," she said fiercely. "But even after this short time I'm not blind about the way you feel towards the Bryants. They're good, honourable people, and. . . ."

". . . and you're in love with one of them."

Unable to bear the sarcastic note in his voice, she stood up and walked quickly away. She must find Donald, she must. She wanted him to be near her, to hold her.

She met him coming up from the beach with Margo trailing behind. Reaching for his hand, she said in a high, quick voice, "I've done all the drawing I'm going to. Isn't it about time we went?"

"I was just thinking the same myself. There's work to be done." But for some strange reason the touch of his hand on hers offered no real comfort.

It was only the following day, when Carrie was out on her rounds, that fate took a hand once more. The little van had not been behaving too well all the morning, so all Carrie hoped was that it would get her home before packing up altogether. But that was not to be. There were only about another four miles to go when the engine huffed and puffed, then died altogether.

She got out, opened the bonnet and peered inside, without any hope of guessing what the trouble was at all. As she straightened wondering what to do, a voice called, "Hi there!" and she looked up to see Harvey Mercer, her young American rescuer, striding across the road.

"Not in trouble again?" he grinned.

"I'm afraid so," she said ruefully. "Do you know

112

anything about cars?"

"A fair amount. It sounds to me like dirty plugs."

"Oh. Then I must either find a garage, or ring the Bryants."

"I have a far better idea." He took her by the arm and led her half protesting across the road. "See, you couldn't have stopped at a better place—the Reef. I'll get one of the chaps here to have a go at the plugs while you and I have a drink. If that doesn't work we'll get on the blower and I'll give you a lift home in our hired mini-moke. O.K.?"

"O.K.," she agreed, laughing. Like many Americans he had the hotel staff organised within minutes and then was leading her through to the terrace overlooking the reef where his father was stretched out on a lounging chair.

"Say, Dad," he poked the older man in the ribs, "I've brought you a visitor."

Mr. Mercer sat up abruptly, but his welcome was as open and warm as his son's.

"Miss Fleming . . . we're delighted to meet up with you again. We were wondering if you'd had any effects from your ducking."

She shook her head. "No, I was fine. But I gather I was very lucky. If I hadn't hit that island, then that would have been that. And I was also lucky to meet you. As it was the people I'm staying with had given me up for drowned."

Within a few minutes there were ice-cold drinks on the table and Carrie was hearing all about their fishing trips, the marlin and the sailfish they had caught off the famous Seychelles Bank and the dolphins they had seen but not caught. There was an openness and an exuberance about these two that Carrie liked even more this second time.

"You must have been everywhere," she laughed.

"Nearly but not quite. We're saving two of the

best until last."

"And where's that?" she asked.

"Praslin and La Digue," said Harvey promptly. "Dad says he isn't going back until he's seen the black parrot in the Vallée de Mai."

"Oh," said Carrie eagerly, "that's just what I want to see. They say both islands are absolutely beautiful."

Father and son looked at each other, then said, almost in a chorus, "Then you must come with us. We'll fix up a party and make a couple of days of it. They say there's a good hotel if you don't want to stay on the boat . . . might even take in Cousin if there's time."

"Wait," Carrie already out of breath, "please wait. I don't know that I could come."

"Why?" said Harvey promptly.

"I . . . I don't know, but the people I'm staying with. . . ."

"Bring them too." Harvey leaned forward. "Look, our boat takes twelve easily. It will be a chance to have a few people who aren't from the hotel—nice crowd though they are. We'll leave it to you to invite a few people and let us know when you want to go—say in a couple of days' time."

Suddenly Carrie was caught up with their enthusiasm. Why not? She might persuade Donald to take a couple of days off, and perhaps even the Raymonds and Margo might like to come. They were always talking about Praslin, saying how rarely they were able to get there.

"Well, what do you say, Miss Fleming?" That was Mr. Mercer this time.

"I say yes," she said, laughing. "At least, I'll do my best and let you know as soon as I can. I must say it sounds fun."

In the end it was Harvey who drove her home,

114

saying he would fix it that the van would be delivered back that afternoon.

She tried to tell them there was no need to take so much trouble, but all Harvey said was, "Aw, hell, we got nothing else to do. Besides, since you won't stay and have lunch with us, I guess you'll want to get back."

Donald must have seen the 'moke' drop her just outside Cinnamon Hill, for he was walking down to meet her as she clambered up the path.

"What happened?" he demanded.

"The van packed up," she explained. "It's all right, don't worry, it's nothing serious, something to do with the plugs. It will be back this afternoon."

"Then who gave you a lift?"

"Those Americans—the Mercers—who brought me back from Tern the other day." She ignored Donald's faint scowl and went on gaily, "They're very kind and very American . . . they've invited you and me, and anyone else who wants to come, for a trip to Praslin."

"I can't take any trips," Donald said sourly, "and you know I don't like you being picked up by anyone."

"They weren't just anyone, Donald," she said patiently, "and at least we're going to talk about the trip. You need to have a couple of days off, you're looking tired and you're getting grouchy. Well, what do you say?"

He broke into a reluctant grin. "You're quite right, I am getting grouchy. We'll talk about it tonight. You and I and the Raymonds are invited to dinner at the Casuarina. Margo is laying on a spread. Do you want to come?"

"If you're going, then yes, I want to come," she said simply.

CHAPTER EIGHT

Margo's dinner party turned out to be one of the highlights of Carrie's stay in the Seychelles. As she had instinctively guessed, it was a somewhat sophisticated affair with all the women in long formal dresses and the men in dark jackets. Apart from Donald and herself and the Raymonds, there were two other couples, both of whom had worked on the island for some years.

The table was laid out on the terrace overlooking the little beach and harbour and the cool evening breeze seemed to lift away the steaming heat of the day. Margo sat at the head of the table, looking even more beautiful than ever, wearing a long white dress of some clinging material, absolutely plain and high at the throat, with her dark, shining hair tumbling about her face. Whenever she talked all eyes were upon her— Donald's too—so that Carrie could not stop herself feeling gauche and inexperienced. She was probably at least six years younger than anyone else present; never had she felt the need for more experience.

Nevertheless, Carrie did enjoy herself, even if she was conscious of being an outsider looking in. The food Margo had prepared was as exotic as the setting, succulent pork in a rich sauce, several varieties of fish, and bowls of salad.

It was Sally Raymond who put Carrie's thoughts into words by saying, as she laid down her fork with a sigh, "I think it's grossly unfair, Margo."

"What is?" the other girl asked.

"That you should not only look as you do, but you should actually be able to cook like this. You wait till we get home and Bill starts to complain that we never had such food!"

Bill grinned at his wife and said, "It wouldn't do any good if I did complain, we'd still have fish and breadfruit chips everyday!"

They all laughed, knowing how utterly devoted the Raymonds were.

Margo, perhaps thinking that Carrie had been left out of things just a little, looked across at her and said, "You've only about ten more days left, Carrie, haven't you, and still so much to see. When is Donald going to get you across to Praslin?"

Feeling Donald glance sharply at her, Carrie said rather shyly, "Donald and I have had an invitation to go to Praslin on a boat belonging to two Americans. They said we could bring some friends and make it a party."

"Not a father and son in that absolutely super boat?" Margo looked quite excited.

Carrie nodded. "That's right. Then you will come?" She turned to the Raymond. "And you too? If you all will come then I think I can persuade Donald to take some time off."

So Donald was reluctantly talked into coming. Even Bill Raymond said he might snatch a couple of days off, since he had not been to Praslin for almost a year, and besides, who could resist a boat like that?

When dinner was over Margo said, before serving coffee, that she must see to her hotel guests, so Carrie found herself persuaded by the Raymonds to walk down to the moonlit beach.

Sally kicked off her shoes and dipped her toes into the creaming surf. "There's something," she sighed, "quite special about a beach at night. It's got a sort of untouched feel about it. I wish we had somewhere like this at the end of our garden."

Carrie felt the sand cool between her toes, watch-

ing the blue-black water stretching out into the distance. She could understand why Donald wanted to
base his business here. Surely, she thought, Jonas
could be persuaded to give in to this. It seemed such
a small favour to ask, and she turned to tell Donald
so, but he was nowhere to be seen. The Raymonds
were there, standing in a little group with the other
four guests, but Donald, whom Carrie had thought
to be just behind her, was not on the beach.

With a queer little twist to her stomach she
looked up towards the flickering lanterns on
the terrace. He was not there either; neither was
Margo. Carrie closed her eyes in sudden pain. Surely
she had been dreaming when she imagined he
looked at Margo in a special way tonight? But then
Bill had too, and the other men. But Margo was
every man's dream . . . why should she have this
awful premonition of danger? It was as though
something told her that Donald and Margo were
being drawn inexorably, unconsciously towards
each other. Was she the only one to see it? And then
she saw Sally look at her and look away. She knows,
Carrie thought fiercely, she knows.

When Margo put her head over the terrace and
called that coffee was ready, Carrie wished she could
go home. But as she hung back after the others,
Donald came down to hustle her along, taking her
by the hand, pushing all her fears away. And for the
rest of the evening he never left her side.

When they arrived back at Cinnamon Hill
Donald held her in his arms and kissed her before
they went inside. Carrie wanted to tell him not to
pretend, that they would not go to Praslin after all,
but she could not find the words. Only when she
was alone in her little white room with the hot night
enfolding her in its cocoon did she decide that attack
was the best form of defence. While most of her

ached to keep Donald and Margo apart, her head told her that she must do the exact opposite. She had exactly ten days in which to find out if Donald really loved her or whether he was wishing for the moon. And she wanted the truth.

On the morning of their departure to Praslin Carrie was up early, a small overnight bag packed and feeling almost happy again, some of the darker fears of the past twenty-four hours having disappeared, with Donald loving and attentive, as carelessly cheerful as he had been in England.

On the verandah, as Ginette laid breakfast in front of her, Mrs. Bryant appeared, her face sombre.

"What is it?" Carrie asked immediately. "Not Mr. Bryant?"

"No, my dear, it's Donald. Oh, nothing serious, just one of the local bugs. He tells me he's been up most of the night."

"Oh, poor Donald!" Carrie was full of concern. "I must go to him."

"Carrie. . . ."

"Yes?" Carrie paused at the door.

"He wants you to go to Praslin with the others. He . . . he's not a very good patient and if he thinks you're staying at home, fretting about him, it will only make him worse."

"But I *couldn't* go without him."

And yet when she saw Donald's form huddled down in the bed and heard his muffled voice telling her he'd be all right in a day or so and that he just wanted to be alone, so would she please go with the others, she knew it was the best thing to do. Nothing was going quite right with this holiday, but it certainly would not make things any better for her to stay at home and mope too, and make Donald feel guilty that he had spoiled yet another trip for her.

She bent and kissed him on the top of his thick

fair hair. "All right," she whispered, "I'll go, but on sufferance, because I shan't enjoy myself without you. I'm going only so that I can say I've been to the islands."

He turned a bleary eye towards her. "Bill and Sally will look after you. As long as you stay clear of those Yanks. . . ."

She smiled. "If there's any trouble, I'll tell them I'm spoken for. That sounds deliciously old-fashioned and English, doesn't it? But they're only interested in the fishing, so you needn't worry." She wanted to say more, to reassure him, but already his head was sunk into the pillow again.

The Raymonds took her by car into Victoria to the yacht harbour where the Mercers were already waiting aboard their cabin cruiser, *Sea Spinner*. Margo was there, and it did not take Carrie more than a moment to see that she had woven her spell over them too. Father and son were practically falling over themselves to see that she was comfortable.

Sally nudged Carrie. "I think Margo is the only person who could really charm the birds off a tree and honestly not know she's doing it. In any other person it would be deliberate flirtation, but not Margo."

"I know," said Carrie quietly, "I've learned that already."

When they were all settled in, Harvey Mercer called out, "Right, are we ready to go?"

They all nodded and Carrie asked, "How long will it take us?"

"A couple of hours, but first Margo wants to pick up her hermit friend."

Carrie flashed a look at Margo sitting next to her and said in a low voice, but with overtones of anger, "You didn't say that Jonas was coming?"

Margo's beautiful eyes were shadowed by huge

120

dark glasses, so Carrie could not read her expression as she said, "No, I didn't think of it until yesterday when I saw one of his boys in town. He's been waiting for a week or two to go to Praslin; there's a house up for sale that I think might make a quiet fishing lodge. So I've suggested he came and look it over. You don't mind, do you? It's Donald who doesn't get on with him, and he's not here."

"But you didn't know Donald was going to be ill. It could have spoilt the trip for all of us."

Margo tilted her head to one side. "If there's one thing I'm determined to do before I'm much older, that's to stop this silly one-sided feud between those two men. Surely you would agree with that?"

"Yes. Yes, I suppose I would," Carrie said reluctantly.

"Well then, don't worry yourself about it. Jonas can look after both of us . . . on second thoughts," and she winked broadly, "I think I shall find my time taken up with Mr. Mercer senior. He says he's going to take me out fishing. I haven't the heart to tell him that I'm reckoned to be quite an expert!"

They anchored off Tern while Jonas came out in the long, double-prowed pirogue. As he climbed aboard, Carrie was surprised to find how pleased she was to see him. He met her glance with that quick, rare smile and she felt ridiculously happy.

The island that Carrie had seen on a fine day from Cinnamon Hill gradually came out of the mist, like a long ragged hill in the middle of the ocean.

As Carrie shaded her eyes to watch it grow nearer, she found Jonas beside her. "They say," he told her, "that when you land on Praslin for the first time you don't want to leave."

She looked sideways at him. "You mean I'll think it more beautiful than Tern?"

He shrugged. "Tern is home. It's an interesting

121

island, but it would never be known for its beauty. Did you know that General Gordon, when he discovered the Vallée de Mai, was quite convinced that Praslin was the original Garden of Eden? People still wax lyrical about it because civilization hasn't truly touched it. There are still only a couple of dozen cars." He shaded his eyes against the sun. "If ever I built a house for myself it would be there, on Praslin."

"I thought you and Margo were going to look at a house?" she remarked.

"A guest house," he corrected her. "Margo is a business woman."

". . . and you're her adviser," Carrie put in.

"Say," called Harvey, "I'm heading for the harbour marked on our charts. Is it the only one?"

Jonas turned to him. "It's the only one for a boat of this size. You'll need to head a little further east in order to find the main passage between the reefs, but once in to St. Anne it's sheltered enough."

Harvey was grinning at Carrie. "Looks a swell little island, eh, Carrie? Too bad your boy-friend couldn't come. As soon as we land Dad and I thought we'd go straight to this famous valley. Going to join us?"

"Please," said Carrie, "that's what I've come for. Jonas here says it's the original Garden of Eden."

For some reason she could not quite fathom, both men burst into laughter.

In the end they all went to the valley. Somehow Jonas organised a large brake which appeared from nowhere as soon as they landed and they all piled in and drove up the hillside round some steep curving roads, to stop in a quiet shady area.

"This it?" queried Mr. Mercer, who seemed to have brought a great deal of photographic equipment.

the coco-de-mer. Sally sniffed at it and wrinkled her nose, but Carrie did not find it anything but rather sweet.

She would like to have stayed on this strange valley, to explore further and in the hope of glimpsing the parrot, but it was obvious the others wanted to get back to the beach to swim and laze in the sun, so with some reluctance she followed them back along the path and eventually out again to the car. After the intense gloom of the forest, the sun struck at them with almost painful intensity.

There was time, before lunch, for a swim from Praslin's most beautiful and popular beach, the Côte d'Or. Afterwards, lying on the beach, Sally murmured to Carrie, "I think this is my favourite beach of all. This is where I would build my dream cottage and just lie here every day watching the birds and the fantastic colour of the sea." She turned sideways to look at Carrie, who was sitting up, hugging her knees, watching a pirogue skimming across the flat blue surface. "There's something else strange today."

"What's that?" Carrie was only half listening.

"Jonas."

Carrie looked down sharply. "Why Jonas? What's wrong with him?"

"Nothing's wrong," Sally said gently, "quite the contrary, in fact. He never comes on outings like this, but if he did he would never behave like a tourist, visiting the Vallée, lying on the beach like this. I don't think I've ever seen him so relaxed."

Carrie glanced across at where Jonas was talking earnestly with Margo. "Perhaps," she said, with some tartness, "he just wants to be treated as an ordinary human being, Even he likes to have company sometimes."

"Now," returned Sally, laughing, "you're talking

125

just like me. I've spent the last two years champion-ing Jonas." She closed her eyes. "The only person—or people—I haven't managed to convert are Donald and his father."

"Perhaps they have a special reason," Carrie said loyally. "You could hardly call Jonas an easy man."

"No, but that's just what makes him interesting. I find him a very interesting man. Attractive too. Don't you?"

Carrie looked again across at the object of their conversation. His black hair fell over his forehead. From here she could not see his expression, but it seemed he was smiling at Margo.

"Yes," she said steadily, "he's a very interesting man. It's a pity that he and Margo. . . ."

"Everyone tries to push them together, but they'll never go," Sally said. "Each of them is too much of an individualist. It's a pity, because Jonas will never admit that he's lonely."

"I gather," Carrie reminded her, "that he doesn't have too much regard for women."

"I know, but Bill and I have told him often enough that all women aren't tarred with the same brush. Ah . . . ." she sat up, "it looks as if lunch is on the cards. I'm starving!"

Leading again, Jonas took them all up a steep, hair-raising road literally hacked out of the hillside, to a small hotel only recently built, owned, he ex-plained, by a friend of his. A small, round house built of granite, with wooden doors and shutters, all open, it commanded a view from every side, towards the coast and down a tree-clad hillside.

Their welcome was warm and they ate a delicious lunch of tuna fish and mango salad, followed by bananas and caramelised paw-paws.

As they sipped their coffee on the open verandah, Harvey, sitting next to Carrie, said in a low voice,

"Your friend Brandon seems to be a bit of a king-pin in these islands. Does he know everyone?"

"Apparently," Carrie smiled.

"I like the fellow, even if he is a bit of a screwball with his birds. Seems to get a lot out of life without much effort." He paused. "Dad was telling me he recognised him as quite a well-known character in motor racing. Is that right?"

"I believe so," Carrie said cautiously. "But Margo's the one to tell you more. I've only met him a few times."

Sensing that she did not want to talk about Jonas, Harvey stretched out his bare toes, saying, "Dad and I want to try the fishing round here for a couple of hours. I think the Raymonds are coming too. How about you?"

Carrie would quite have enjoyed fishing, but she remembered there would be the journey back to-morrow morning. "I think," she said politely, "if you don't mind, I'd like to potter about here a bit, see a little more of the island, perhaps do some sketching."

Margo overheard her decision. "We can't leave you on your own, Carrie. Come with Jonas and me. It's a business trip, but we could leave you on the beach while we talk."

Carrie shook her head. Even if she wasn't playing gooseberry she would have felt like it. "Honestly, I'm quite happy on my own. I might go for a walk, or even back to the Vallée de Mai."

So it was arranged that they would all meet back here at about six o'clock, when darkness fell. Jonas had somehow managed to book them all rooms, so there was not even any need for the Mercers to sleep on their boat.

Carrie watched them all go and as Jonas turned round she thought for a moment he was going to try to persuade her to come, but then he half smiled, as if he understood anyone wanting to be alone.

For a little while Carrie stayed around, drinking an extra cup of coffee, her sketch pad on her knee, amusing herself with the hotel's pet pig, a tiny friendly animal, who obviously did not like being alone. When she decided to walk down the steep path to the beach, it tried to follow her, and had to be forcibly restrained by one of the hotel staff, amid loud squeals.

As she sat under the palms listening to the noisy, quarrelling fairy terns flying about above her, watching the changing patterns of the seaweed as the monsoon tide tossed it up on the beach, it occurred to her with a shock that she had not thought of Donald since she left this morning. She wondered if he were feeling better, if he had really wanted to come.

The days were flying by, in the inevitable way of all holidays, after the first few leisurely days. In another week, if not before, Donald would be wanting her answer, and she was no more ready to give it now than she had been when she arrived. In fact, if anything, her doubts had gathered strength, for there had been so many sharp words.

I should never have come, she thought in sudden panic. I would somehow have forgotten Donald in time, as though our swift loving had been only a holiday romance, of no lasting consequence. Now, in a way, I'm committed, and afraid.

She stood up quickly, wanting to drive the thoughts of Donald and her decision from her mind. She should have gone fishing, after all. With the others there would have been no time for thought, but there was still nearly two hours before they would return.

When she climbed back to the hotel again, she

saw that one of the staff was backing out of the precarious drive. On impulse she said to him, "Are you going anywhere near the Vallée de Mai?"

"Right past it. Do you want a lift?"

"Please," she said. "Can you give me just two minutes to change my shoes and collect my things?"

She replaced trousers and long-sleeved shirt and grabbed her pad and pencils before running back to the car.

The young man grinned. "I suppose you're going to try to see the black parrot?"

"Yes. Do you think there's any chance?"

"Well, let's say this is the best time of day. I've taken people and seen four, and nothing for a couple of weeks. It's a matter of luck." He squinted at the sky. "But we might be in for a shower."

Carrie laughed. "I don't think it would be possible to get wet in there. Does the rain ever get through all those leaves?"

"No, but it makes a hell of a noise trying."

When Carrie entered the silent gloom of the Vallée again, she was very conscious of being on her own. Quite obviously there would be no more tourist parties today. She plunged down the path, retracing some of the morning's walk, but wanting to go even further. Suddenly she heard a call, loud in the silence, '*wheet-whoit-whoit*,' and knew without a shadow of a doubt that it was the black parrot she was hearing. She followed the sound which seemed to be even ahead of her, just off the path, watching up in the trees for the smallest movement that would indicate the bird's presence. And then there was an answering call, and she knew she was looking for a pair.

Funny, she thought, screwing up her eyes, it seems to be much darker than this morning. Presumably, at this end, the foliage was even denser.

After a while the calls stopped and she knew with disappointment that she was not going to see the rare black parrot today. She had better go back and somehow make her way to the hotel.

Carrie turned on her tracks, but soon came to a fork and hesitated. She had been so busy following the parrots that she had taken little notice of the way she had come. All she could remember from this morning was that there were several paths, some leading nowhere but only one to the exit.

She paused. It really was not her imagination, but darkness was falling. Perhaps when the sun went down, or the sky clouded over, it had its own effect in her. Then, glancing at her watch, she saw that it was five-thirty. In another half hour it would be true darkness.

I must get out of here, she thought, remembering all the Praslin superstitions of being in the Vallée after dark. She stood for a moment trying to get some idea of her bearings, but then realised she had not the faintest idea in which direction to start walking. She was well and truly lost.

CHAPTER NINE

Carrie was not immediately scared, only annoyed that once again she had behaved stupidly. The only thing she could do, she decided, was to follow the path she was on until it came to a turning, and then she would make some kind of mark so as not to take the same path again. In that way, she must get out in the next half hour.

At the first fork she drew on the ground with a heavy stick and walked on. It seemed to be getting dark with appalling speed. At that moment there was a clap like thunder and Carrie stopped, gasping aloud, until she realised it was only one of the leaves falling.

In the last few minutes a wind must have sprung up, because the valley was no longer silent, and the noise of the huge leaves clashing together was like the metallic sound of one corrugated iron roof rubbing against another. At each bend in the path she felt she was being followed, but when she turned there was, of course, no one there, only the harsh rustling of a million dead and forgotten leaves.

By the time a new sound joined the others Carrie could only admit she was afraid. At first she did not know what it was and stood cowering against the vast trunk of a palm tree, listening to something like rapid fire from a machine gun, until, with only a small sense of relief, she realised she was hearing rain, slamming down on the leaves a hundred feet above her.

She felt she must have been walking for an hour, stumbling on, feeling her way through almost total darkness. The only way she was guided was the fact that if she did step off the path she knew it in no uncertain terms, for her foot seemed to sink down through all those layers of crackling leaves. It was like being in a maze, circling, turning, up and down with nothing to indicate in which way she was walking. Even the fact that she knew there was no known danger here did not make her any the less afraid.

In the end she stubbed her toes hard on a piece of rock and found at least it was somewhere to sit. And so she crouched there, wondering if this was where she was going to spend the night, and if it was, whether she would survive it in her right mind.

When she heard the shout she thought she must be dreaming and did not even look up. But when it came again and she heard 'Carrie . . . Carrie!' echoing through the cavernous forest then she jumped up filled with hope.

"Hello!" she yelled. "Hello!" but she did not move. It could be just a dream . . . if could be all her fears and hopes calling out to her. Only when she saw and recognised the distant beam of a flashlight did she know that rescue was truly at hand and start to walk towards it.

"Carrie, Carrie!" It was clear now and she was able to answer:

"I'm here, just here!"

Out of the darkness came a tall, lean figure, and then she was running.

The next moments were a blur. She only knew that she was crying, that Jonas's arms were about her, soothing her, telling her she was safe now, and that she wanted to stay pressed against the cool cotton shirt.

After a long time he moved, letting his fingers gentle away the damp tendrils of her hair.

"Don't cry any more, Carrie, please don't cry. I can't bear it. You sound so unhappy and frightened, and yet you're really and truly safe."

"I know I am," she whispered. "It's just that I'm so confused. I can't help myself."

"Come with me," and he took her hand and led her, not too far along the path, up a steep slope to an open shelter with a thatched roof and plain wooden seats that she remembered seeing that morning.

She looked up and could see the sky at last. A deep velvety blue, sprinkled with stars and with the moon just coming up. There was even the smallest of breezes to cool the thick air rising from the Vallée.

Jonas pushed her gently on to one of the wooden benches. "You see," he said, pointing up to the sky, "you really are out of it."

Carrie shivered. "I know there was no danger, but I was beginning to think I was in some kind of tomb . . . being buried alive or something."

He was smiling. "It takes a very brave person to stay in the Vallée after dark and not feel the fear of never seeing the light again." He paused. "What made you go back?"

"I wanted to see the black parrot," she said helplessly, "and do some drawing. I didn't mean to stay more than a half hour, but it started to get dark and then for a little while there was rain. It was . . . was like bullets on a tin roof."

"I know. At least I've been there in the rain. You should have told someone, Carrie."

"There was no one to tell," she said in a low voice, "except the boy who drove me."

" . . . who was just off to the other side of the island. It was a good job someone saw you getting into the car and I was able to track him down."

"You mean . . ." she looked at him, puzzled, "you really were worried?"

"Worried? I was out of my mind," he said savagely. "At first there appeared to be no trace of you

133

at all from when you vanished from the hotel. You silly, foolish little thing!"

"I'm sorry," she said with great dignity, "I caused you so much trouble. You should have left me. I've no doubt I would have found my way out eventually."

"Oh, God, Carrie, it's not the *trouble* you caused I'm grumbling at. Can't you see what I'm trying to tell you?"

She shook her head mutely.

"Perhaps this will help."

Suddenly his arms were round her again, crushing her until she felt there was no breath left in her body. And then his mouth was on hers, gentle at first, then with mounting passion until she felt her own heart soaring to meet his. His hands were running through her hair and she felt the pounding of his heart against hers.

"*Now* do you understand?" he cried at last, pushing her away from him, but still holding tightly to her.

"Oh, yes," she whispered, "I understand, but I can only think I must be dreaming. You . . . Jonas Brandon . . . feeling like that towards me? I'm just a girl who seemed to be intruding on all your privacy."

"And thank God you did. I think I really fell in love with you the moment I saw you lying on my beach and I thought you were dead. I suddenly realised that if I wasn't careful, against you I was going to be utterly defenceless. Oh, I tried, I tried very hard, but time is running out, and then this evening, when I knew you must be in here, frightened and probably very lost, I knew I could keep silent no longer."

Carrie did not know what to say. She only knew that her whole body was tingling, that she would turn away from him, but yet she had no power to do so.

Only when he reached out a hand to raise her to her feet, saying, "Come on, I'm taking you back to the Hotel. I shouldn't have kept you in this place."

"I'm not afraid. Not now," she said simply. "I . . . I think I'm just a bit muddled, Jonas."

"Of course you are." He bent to kiss her lightly. "It's been a long time since I've acted—and spoken —so instinctively. We'll talk later."

"I don't think . . ." she started.

"Oh, we have to talk, Carrie, you know that."

She nodded, but all the time she was trying to push to the back of her mind more decisions she would have to make.

Fortunately, when they reached the hotel again the others were all there and anxious to hear about her spooky experiences in the Vallée.

"Did you actually mean to stay there after dark?" Sally said, aghast. "As far as I know no one has deliberately gone in there on their own."

"Of course I didn't," Carrie laughed uneasily, "I'm not half as brave. I just didn't dream it could be so difficult to find the way out. It was like being in a maze."

"And you saw the black parrots?" Harvey asked eagerly.

"Alas, no, I only heard them—that was the start of my troubles, trying to follow the sound so that I really could see them."

From then on until after dinner, there was no opportunity to be alone with Jonas. They were a gay and lively party, with the two Americans insisting on cracking a couple of bottles of champagne. They told crazy stories of their fishing trips and their travels all over the world while the Raymonds laughed and Jonas listened, his smoke-dark eyes

135

never revealing his innermost thoughts.

It was as though, Carrie decided, he had never spoken like that a couple of hours ago, Perhaps, she thought wildly, he had not. Perhaps that had been all a dream too.

The only thing was, once or twice during dinner, Carrie felt Margo's eyes on her, as though in an extra-perceptive way she knew something had happened. But she said little until after dinner, yawning, she stretched and said, "I'd forgotten how tiring it was to have a day off. I think I'll turn in early. All this fresh air has gone straight to my head."

The Raymonds were next to go and after that the Mercers said they wanted to check the boat down in the harbour. It was as though it was all a ruse to leave Carrie and Jonas alone together.

Carrie stood up quickly. "I think I ought to go to bed too."

"You're on holiday," he pointed out. "There's no excuse of 'back to work' tomorrow. Besides, we're going to walk down to the beach. It will clear our heads after all that champagne."

It was a rough path down, but his hand was always there to steady her. He said little, as though he were allowing her time to collect her thoughts, but when they had reached the soft warm sand of the beach and there was no sound but the breeze touching the fronds of the palms he said, "One day, Carrie, I'm going to take you over to the west of Mahé and show you the green flash."

"The green flash?" She tilted her head to one side. "What's that?"

"It's something you can only see under certain weather conditions. When the sun dips right down over the horizon on an absolutely clear evening, it goes through all the colours of the spectrum. Once in a while as the green appears to touch the water there's a great blaze of green fire. It only lasts a couple of seconds, but it's worth going a long way to see. Carrie?"

"Yes?" She turned to him, smiling, expecting perhaps another neutral question. But she was quite wrong.

"Are you in love with Donald?"

Caught completely off guard, Carrie sat down abruptly on a lump of smooth rock. It was a question she had been afraid to ask herself for days now, for fear of the answer. She could not possibly lie to this man who was so direct and honest himself, but equally, could she tell him the truth?

Without doubt she knew she did not love Donald. At least in a way she did love him, as she had wanted to love him back in England, but that was not the same as being totally in love. She had never understood the fine distinction, but now she did.

"I want an answer, Carrie."

"You have no right. . . ."

"I have all the rights of any man in love to ask that question."

Carrie put her arms across herself as if she were cold, but she still did not answer.

"All right, Carrie." He sat down beside her and although she did not look at him, she knew what expression there was in his eyes. She was beginning to know that very well. "I'm going to ask you something else."

She waited.

"Ever since I first saw you at the airport I've known you were afraid of something—of loving, of being too close, I don't know what it is, but it's all there in the way you look at me, even when you look at Donald. I've never asked you about your other life in England, but now I want you to tell me. Will you do that?"

"There's nothing to tell," she said in a low voice. "At least to me my life has been very dull."

"But not happy?"

"I think," she said, "I stopped being really happy when I was fourteen. At that point my parents quarrelled and went to live apart. You think you're quite grown up at fourteen, but nothing prepared me for the shock, because there had never been any signs of it—or if there were they'd hidden them all from me. After about a year they divorced. My mother went to live in America finally and she married again. My father lived on his own and then with his sister. I seemed always being squeezed in somewhere where I wasn't really wanted. Oh, I don't mean people weren't kind, but there was never anywhere I could call my own, and though Father still loved me, he was sort of remote, as though all the stuffing had been knocked out of him. He died about two years ago. I honestly believe he died of a broken heart. He never recovered from the break-up of his marriage."

"My poor Carrie, poor storm-tossed Carrie!"

"What happened to me," she said sturdily, "is no worse than what happens to a thousand other girls, it's just that it forced me to stand on my own feet and, more than anything else, that when I marry it has to be for keeps."

"No one can offer you a guarantee of that, Carrie."

"I know." There was a catch in her voice. "But at least *I* have to be sure."

"Was there anyone before Donald?"

She nodded. "He died." She hoped he would not ask about David. That was a closed book.

He did not, but he did go back to his first question. "Carrie, are you going to tell me about Donald?"

She bent her head very low. "I won't be marrying him. I should never have come out here, I know that now. I've taken love and kindness under false pretences."

"Oh, Carrie, Carrie, you do really want to take the guilt of the world on your shoulders! Had Donald's parents lived, say, in Brighton, and you'd been invited, you would probably have got on a train and gone home as soon as you discovered the truth about your feelings, but here you can't do that, you have to wait until your particular plane lands in a week's time. Mrs. Bryant will understand, she's that sort of woman."

"But Donald won't."

After that they were both silent, knowing she spoke the truth.

"And there's another thing," Carrie said sadly. "Every stroke of bad luck that Donald has had he seems to connect with you. If I let him down now. . . ."

Suddenly she knew what she had to do. It was not going to be easy, but if she did otherwise too many people were going to be hurt. She stood up, brushing the sand off her skirt.

"Jonas, I'm tired, I really would like to go back and to bed. It's been a very long day."

"We haven't talked about us, Carrie."

"There's nothing to talk about," she said coolly. "I made a fool of myself in the Vallée, and you've been very . . . very tolerant towards me. That's all."

"That damn well isn't all!" he came back harshly, standing over her, his eyes so piercing in the moonlight that she had to look away. "Some time ago I told you I loved you. I'm now saying it again. In the Vallée I felt your response. Are you telling me that meant nothing?"

"Nothing," she said in the same, cool, clipped

voice. "Nothing at all. I was very frightened and I think I would have flung myself into the arms of anyone who had happened to turn up then— Harvey, his father, even Bill. I'm afraid you were imagining things."

"Look at me, Carrie." His hands were gripping her shoulders and he forced her to turn right round so that their eyes were locked in combat.

"Well?" she said.

"I think you're lying, Carrie."

Carrie knew she could not keep this up much longer. She took a deep breath. "I'm sorry, Jonas, that you should think that, but it won't make any difference. In a week I shall be gone from the Seychelles and you'll never see me again. I shall always remember how kind you were to teach me so much about the birds. That's all I'll remember."

His hands fell from her shoulders and she knew that barb had gone home. It was a hurtful thing to say but she could think of no other way. When she started to walk up the steep path he made no move to stop her.

Outside the still open terrace she stopped for a moment and turned towards him, although she could not bring herself to look him straight in the eye.

"Good night, Jonas. And thank you again for coming to my rescue in the Vallée de Mai." She walked on towards her room and he made no attempt to call her back.

Once on her own all pretence fell away from her. She started to shake all over and could not stop. When she finally flung herself on the bed she wept and wept, as if she knew for her the end of the world had come.

In the morning Carrie was awake by six, feeling she

had not slept at all, yet knowing she must have done. She felt as limp as a rag-bag, but knowing the Mercers wanted to leave fairly early she decided to get up and have a quick dip in the pool.

Harvey was there before her.

"Hi," he said, "don't say you couldn't sleep either?"

"I . . . I just woke early," Carrie said evasively as she came up from a shallow dive.

"Must be the air here," he said, "it's good and fresh. No ill effects from yesterday?"

"No." Carrie shook her head.

"Your friend Brandon couldn't wait. I saw him leave just as I got up. Seems he remembered some urgent business and got an early lift with one of the local fishing boats. Pity," he grinned, "I was hoping he might invite us to set foot on his island."

"I don't think he would mind," Carrie said quietly, "particularly after all your kindness. But perhaps another time. . . ." So there was to be no morning confrontation. She would not have to go or pretending, or play-acting. Yet at the same time, the thought that she might never see him again left her with a sense of desolation.

They were away before eight, moving sleekly out of the little harbour, that was still as peacefully undisturbed at when they arrived. There were two pirogues heading for the open sea, otherwise the only craft to be seen were two or three sailing boats at anchor, moving slightly on the morning swell.

Carrie sat in the stern, watching the humpy outline of the island grow blurred in the morning haze. In spite of what had happened yesterday she would have dearly loved to return. It seemed to offer the sort of utter tranquillity she had not known for years.

She felt someone move up and sit beside her.

Margo took her huge sunglasses off and said, "Did you like Praslin, Carrie?"

"Yes, I'm sorry to leave."

"I don't know what made Jonas disappear this morning without a word to anyone. You were probably the last to see him last night. Did he say anything?"

Carrie shook her head, not trusting herself to speak.

"Ah, well, that's my brother-in-law for you. Awkward when he wants to be, soft as butter at sometimes and at others. . . ."

"At others?" Carrie prompted.

"Plain mysterious." She half turned away so that Carrie could not see her expression. "You know he's changed his mind about the yacht marina at the Casuarina Hotel? He told me so yesterday. If we want to, Donald and I can go ahead with the sailing project and use the harbour as a base. What do you make of that?"

"When did he tell you?" Carrie said in a tight voice.

"Oh, during the afternoon, when we went to look at this hotel, which, incidentally, wasn't the slightest bit of use. He said it so casually that I thought I wasn't hearing right. I wish I knew what made him change his mind."

Carrie found she was holding her breath. Now she released it slowly. For some reason it was terribly important that Jonas had not changed his mind about the marina *after* he had spoken to her late last night. She might have felt he was offering her some sort of bribe.

"Do *you* know?" Margo said suddenly.

"No, I don't." Carrie was able to answer with complete honesty. She paused. "Donald will be pleased. I don't think he thought that Jonas would give way on anything. May I tell him when we get back . . . or did you want to do that yourself?"

"No, you tell him," said Margo. "It will cheer him up. He might even be able to start making plans—you too. After all, when you and he get married, you'll be part of the travel business as well, won't you?"

"Yes," said Carrie before she could stop herself.

Whether there was a hint of her doubt in her voice, she did not know, but Margo was certainly staring at her. Carrie, hunched up against the wind that was ripping off the stern, surprised a look in Margo's eyes she did not recognise. It was as if a mask had been briefly torn away to reveal . . . she did not know what, but a person who was much more vulnerable than she ever allowed anyone to guess. It was not only Jonas who was lonely but Margo as well.

With the favourable tide they were anchoring in Mahé in record time. There were goodbyes from the Mercers who exacted promises from the others that they would come and dine at the Reef Hotel before the end of the week. Carrie would have liked to ask them to come to Cinnamon Hill, if only for a drink, but she felt it would be imposing. So with more thanks and yet another farewell, she got into the back of the Raymonds' car.

"What nice people," remarked Sally. "And generous, like so many Americans."

"I gather," put in Bill, "they would like to have some sort of stake in the Seychelles. They may be extending their stay to have a look round. They've got sort of hooked on the place."

"Like we are," Sally smiled at him. "And you, Carrie?" She turned her head to the back seat.

"Yes, I'm falling under the spell," agreed Carrie. *Only I have to go and never return.*

She wished suddenly she could confide in Sally, but it would be impossible. The other girl was a neighbour of Donald's and friend of Jonas. It would be too much of a burden for her to bear. No, if she told anyone before she left, surprisingly it would be Margo. And that was because life had been tough with Margo, therefore she probably expected nothing of it, and would never try to offer advice unless asked.

"I hope Donald is better," Sally remarked as they came round the point and saw the ragged outlines of Cinnamon Hill, "If there's anything we can do, let us know."

"I will," Carrie persuaded them to drop her outside their house, so that she could make her own way across to the rambling white house.

As she trudged up the rough track instinctively she pushed the sunglasses down over her eyes, as if she believed that Donald should somehow see into her heart and know of her betrayal.

For a moment she hesitated outside, then, before she could change her mind, she pushed the swing door and went into the house.

CHAPTER TEN

Carrie heard Donald's voice right away. He called, "Is that you, Mother . . . could you lend me a hand?"

She put her head round the door. "It's me, Donald, I'm back. How are you?"

He was sitting on a low chair and all about him were spread bits of an engine. At least that was what it looked like to her. His face was still pale, but he did not look as ghastly as he had when she left yesterday.

"Carrie, darling Carrie!" His welcoming smile made her feel even more treacherous. "Never has anything quite so good walked through that door. First, will you hold this so that I can get the spanner round it."

She did as she was told, saying again, "You haven't told me if you're feeling better."

He pulled a face. "Well, let's say I'm not ready to run the round-the-island race. But at least my stomach has stopped surging. It seems like a week since you went, not just a day." He looked at her. "Don't I get a kiss?"

"Of course." He leaned towards her and their lips met in a light kiss.

Carrie nodded at all the nuts and bolts around him. "What's this?"

"Just one more disaster." He sighed. "The cultivator has packed up now. I thought if I could take the thing to pieces myself I might be able to put it right in half the time the garage would, but I'm not having much luck. Anyway, enough about Cinnamon Hill's problems—how was Praslin?"

"I thought it was just beautiful," Carrie said simply. "Don't ask me to compare it with Mahé, be-

145

cause I think it's all just like paradise, but I suppose to local people it must seem like a haven of peace."

"And the Vallée de Mai, with its erotic coco-de-mer?" he grinned at her.

"Fascinating, but creepy." Carrie was not going to say anything about her experiences, but then she realised that Donald would be certain to hear about it from either Margo or the Raymonds, so she added, "I even got stuck in there after dark. *And* it rained. So I won't be trying anything like that again."

To her surprise all he said was: "Then you're a lot braver than the locals, that's all I can say. Here, hold this again, Carrie, will you."

For a moment he frowned in concentration as he struggled with the job in front of him. For a moment he seemed to have forgotten that she was there and she found herself watching him as if seeing him for the first time. She tried to will herself to make her heart tip over as it had done in London, but she felt nothing, only an odd affection, as if he were an old and dear friend.

Carrie realised that she must accept the truth that she had not faced right from the moment of her arrival. Donald was not for her. Of course, the whole point of her coming all this way was a kind of trial and it was as well to find out now, before even an engagement, that there was no future for them.

But why, she asked herself, why? She had never believed that people could fall in love one moment, then out again the next. Unless . . . she thought about it a little more. Donald had come on the scene in London just when she was getting over David's death. She was ready to fall in love. She *wanted* to fall in love. And Donald, with his easy-going ways, his exuberance, the very fact that he came from a different part of the world, all these had added to his glamour. There had been no time in London to

146

do anything but be happy together. There were no problems, no difficulties, nothing to make them realize the small incompatibilities in each other's personality. She had no idea then that Donald was jealous, even that he was occasionally moody, most of all that he wanted to possess her, to lay down his own rules for the sort of person he wanted her to be.

"You're staring at me," he said suddenly. He was looking at her, faintly puzzled, as if he could half see into mind.

"In Praslin?" he shot at her.

"No," she answered stiffly. "As a matter of fact I was thinking about England, what a long way away it seems, almost like another life. Donald. . . ."

"Yes?"

Carrie swallowed. No, she could not tell him at the moment that she was not going to marry him, that if only she could get a flight home she would leave tomorrow. She had not the courage for that.

"I . . . I've forgotten to give you the good news."

"Good news?" he growled. "I've almost forgotten what that is. Go on, surprise me."

"Margo told me on the way over that Jonas Brandon has given in over the yacht marina at the Casuarina. Apparently you can go ahead if you want to."

He dropped the nut he was holding. "You're joking!" He was staring at her, as if doubting what he had heard.

She shook her head. "No, I'm not joking. She would have told you herself, but she had to dash back to the hotel. Anyway, she thought it might cheer you up."

"Cheer me up? If I felt a bit better I'd get up and shout it from the rooftops!" He suddenly leaned forward and hugged her. "Carrie, I think we're going to be in business. I feel better already."

147

She tried to smile, to join in his pleasure, but all she could think of was that he was more exicted by this news than by the fact she had come back.

Carrie got clumsily to her feet. "I'll go and put my things away, Donald, and then go and find your mother to tell her I'm back. Can I get you anything first?"

"No, nothing, thanks. I'm still off food and Ginette brought me a drink some time ago. Carrie . . ." At the doorway she stopped and turned back. "You *are* pleased, aren't you? It really is the best news I've had for ages. I wonder what made him change his mind. There must be more in it than meets the eye. I reckon Jonas Brandon never does anything without a reason. He's so twisted up inside. . . ."

"Isn't it enough to know that he *has* changed his mind," Carrie said sharply, "without looking into his motives? No one is all bad, you know."

"Maybe, but there are some people you don't actually have to like. Anyway, he seems to have found a champion in you, Carrie."

"That's not fair, Donald," she said hotly, "you know it's not fair. I've told you before, I've got no quarrel with Jonas Brandon . . ." she stopped abruptly and sighed. "There we go again! I simply refuse to quarrel about him. Margo respects him. Doesn't that mean anything to you?"

But she didn't wait for a reply. Donald was absorbed again, or perhaps he simply did not want to listen.

When Carrie had washed and changed she wandered out to the garden with the intention of walking down to the beach before lunch to try to think things over. There was almost another week before she returned home and no other flight to London before then. How could she possibly stay at Cinnamon Hill? Alternatively, where could she go? Until she decided this she felt unable to tell Donald she could not marry him.

She stood for a moment in the heavy morning heat looking out across the dreamless sea. It was a clear day and she could see the outline of Tern Island, its small humpy shape just coming over the horizon. It would be so easy to sail over there and tell Jonas that she longed, more than anything else, to be with him, but she could never do that. It was bad enough to break Donald's heart, but then to flaunt her new love—the one man in the world he despised—would be an intolerable decision. She could never live with herself. Therefore she had to go home and start again. She had done it before, she could undoubtedly learn to do it again. When she looked again into the distance she thought a mist had come up. But it was only her eyes clouded with unshed tears.

Instead of walking down to the beach she turned along the path that led through the banana plants and up towards the pig unit. Above that lay the mountain and some blessed cool. Today the heat seemed to be worse than ever and full of unshed moisture.

She did not think there was anyone about until she walked past the area that had been set aside as a nursery garden, where all the seedlings were and where the more delicate of plants could be kept under a rough shelter of palm fronds, cool and damp and away from the worst of the sun. At a movement she turned her head and stopped in her tracks. Her head in her hands, slumped on an old log, was Mrs. Bryant.

For just a second Carrie hesistated. Perhaps, if there was something wrong, the older woman would prefer to be left alone. On the other hand, she would never forgive herself if she walked past someone who really needed help.

"Mrs. Bryant," she said softly, "it's me, Carrie."

The beautiful, mobile face looked up and today, Carrie saw, it was haggard and very nearly old.

"Oh, Carrie, that you should find me like this! But—well, I'm at my wits' end."

Carrie went and knelt beside her. "Please tell me, what is it?"

"I think we've come to the end of the road. I've been looking into figures and I just simply don't think Cinnamon Hill can survive as it is.. The rain hasn't come, half the seedlings have died. . . ."

"But . . . but we've been watering those," said Carrie.

"They cut off the water yesterday and today. Oh, it's something that happens on this island, but never at such a crucial stage. I can't save them. But that's only one of the problems. I'm just trying to work out how to tell Oliver and Donald the next bit of bad news."

"What's that?" Carrie asked.

"I think one of the pigs has got swine fever. In fact, I know it in my bones. It means the whole lot will have to be slaughtered. And we put our last bit of capital into that unit, because that, we were convinced, was going to put us on our feet."

"Oh, no!" Carrie's own problems suddenly seemed small in the face of all this. "But what will this mean?"

The older woman shook her head. "I don't honestly know," she said, "but I can't see us staying on here. And of course, we have nothing to sell. We could be back where we were nearly thirty years ago. Oliver and I have been through many problems, and somehow we've come through them all, but I don't see what we can do about this. You can't make things grow that don't want to grow. As to Jonas Brandon . . . well, he's going to be proved right after all." She smiled briefly. "I don't think Donald will ever forgive him for that." She suddenly sat up straight and patted Carrie's hand. "Don't look like that, my dear. It isn't really the end of the world. At least we have one thing to be thankful for."

Carrie tried to match her smile. "And what's that?"

"That Donald met you and brought you here. I've enjoyed having a daughter this past two weeks more than I've enjoyed anything for a long time. You've helped to make the burden easier. And as for Donald. . . ."

Carrie waited, not daring to look at her in case her eyes gave her away.

"I think you're the best thing that's happened to Donald for a long time. I don't know what he would do if you were to go now. People always think because Donald is a big strong-looking man, he can stand alone, but he needs someone beside him. I've discovered that ever since he came back from England."

In a very low voice Carrie said, "I'm not altogether sure that I'm the right person for Donald. There's so little I can do to help him."

"Except be with him. The rest will come in time."

It seemed to Carrie, after talking to Mrs. Bryant, that she was more confused than ever. Even less now could she break the news to Donald that she could not marry him. She closed her eyes. Perhaps, she thought, she *ought* to marry him. If she had loved him once then surely she could love him again. Time could heal so many wounds. And if he were counting on her as much as Mrs. Bryant said. . . .

But then Carrie remembered that Jonas was living across the water. On every clear day when she got up in the morning she would see Tern Island and remember that he had kissed her and told her he loved her. If only there was someone to whom she could unburden herself, someone who could perhaps make her see things straight. But in the end her problem could only be solved by herself.

As Carrie went about that day, doing what chores she could, it seemed to her the heart had gone out of Cinnamon Hill. There was quiet everywhere, from inside the house where both Donald and his father rested and even outside. The whirr of the hoses was silenced, one of the men was off sick and where Mrs. Bryant often sang about the work she loved so much, today there was only the sound of crickets and the occasional noisy passing of a local bus on the road below.

Somehow, Carrie determined, she was going to help. She was not going to leave this island without feeling she had done all she could to lift this burden from the Bryants. She thought of Jane Bryant's words of that morning, ". . . the daughter I've enjoyed having these past two weeks." The sad thing was that Carrie would like to have told her truthfully that she was the sort of mother-in-law she had dreamed of having.

By the following morning she had pulled herself together a little, although still not made any decision. But at least today Donald was back doing light work. Perhaps she would tell him tomorrow.

Without any fuss she took over the deliveries again and by mid-morning was turning down the bumpy track that led in to the Casuarina Hotel.

"Hi," said Margo, appearing from the dark of the kitchen, "coffee's just on the boil, or is it fruit juice

152

today?"

"Fruit juice, please," said Carrie. "I thought I was quite good at coping with the heat, but today is almost too much for me." Gratefully she picked up the glass and followed Margo round to the terrace, which at least was shady, and where a small breeze rose from the sea.

"How's Donald?" said Margo.

"Better. Lots better. And what's made all the difference is the news about the marina."

"I know. I talked to him on the phone last night," said Margo casually, "he seemed pretty excited then." She turned to Carrie and regarded her for a moment through her huge sunglasses. "And you," she said abruptly, "are you excited? After all, I suppose you'll be helping to run things until we get on our feet."

Carrie put her glass down carefully on the small iron table, taking one of her impulsive decisions as she did so.

"No," she said quietly, "I won't be helping to run things. I . . . I've decided I can't marry Donald after all."

Margo was very still, but the expression in her eyes was hidden.

"Why?"

"Because I don't love him enough, I suppose," Carrie said simply. And when Margo made no comment she felt impelled to go on: "I suppose I never really was in love with him, it was just a sort of holiday infatuation in London. The trouble is I don't know how I'm going to tell him."

"I suppose there's someone else?"

"*No!*" Carrie lied. Then, wanting to sound less fierce and positive, she said again in a steadier voice, "No, there's no one else. I'll be catching my flight back to London. If I could go earlier I would. That's

153

why I'm scared to tell Donald—because I have to stay on at Cinnamon Hill."

"You could come here for the last few days," Margo said calmly.

Carrie looked at her. She had not thought of anything as simple as this. Then she frowned. "You . . . you don't sound surprised at my decision."

"I'm not. I knew you and Donald weren't right for each other the moment I saw you. Oh, please don't take offence. I like you, Carrie, I like you very much, but . . . well, I think you're too gentle for Donald. You care too much about things. Donald wants to make a big name for himself, *be* someone in the world, but I don't think that's terribly important to you. You're more . . . more Jonas's sort of person."

Carrie drew in her breath sharply and shot a look at Margo. Margo had taken off her glasses and was returning that look with bland innocence. Surely she could not have guessed? No, Carrie decided, hoping her own expression had not given her away, no; all Margo was trying to say was that she and Jonas appreciated the same kind of things, the birds, the wild beauty of the islands, the ordinary simple things that money cannot buy.

She drank the last of her fruit juice and rose quickly. "Well, I think I'd better be on my way. I . . . I'm glad I talked to you, it's sort of cleared my mind."

Margo smiled. "But you haven't answered my question."

"I'm sorry, I don't understand."

"I mean," said Margo, "do you want to come here?"

"Perhaps," answered Carrie. "I think I must leave it until I do talk to Donald. If I do turn up with my suitcase, then I hope there'll still be room for me."

"There will, I promise."

It was while Carrie was driving home, through the outskirts of Victoria, that she saw a smiling Seychellois boy waiting to cross the road. She took her foot off the throttle, thinking, where have I seen him before? And then, in a flash, she realised it was Johnny, the boy from Tern Island.

She pulled up with a jerk, jumped out of the car and ran back to him.

"Hello, Johnny."

"Hello, miss." The huge beam grew even wider.

"Johnny, is Mr. Brandon with you?"

"No, miss, I'm by myself."

"Are you going back to Tern?"

He nodded. "This afternoon."

"Then will you wait five minutes while I write a note to Mr. Brandon for you to take?"

She went back and rummaged in the car pocket and found an old postcard with the back plain. She wrote as the words came, hardly stopping to think, but telling him about the Bryants' plight, begging him to do something to help them when the time came, which she was sure would, after she had gone back to England. She did not mention Donald, nor did she refer to their own brief relationship, only thanking him formally and telling him once more that she would be returning to England within a few days.

She hovered over the last sentence. She so badly wanted to say something warm, something that would perhaps show him at least she cared. But no, she dared not, for her heart would so easily give her away, so she just signed it briefly, informally, 'with good wishes, Carrie', and before she could change her mind she handed it to Johnny.

"You will give it to Mr. Brandon today, won't you?" she said. "It is rather important."

"Oh, yes, miss, I give it to him as soon as I get back." He shook his head suddenly. "But Mr. Brandon not like himself today and yesterday."

"What do you mean?" Her voice was full of fear. "Is he ill?"

"Oh no, Mr. Brandon not *ill*. But he is sick, here," and very dramatically he put his brown hand over his heart. "He does not talk, he does not laugh." His own smile had vanished as he obviously thought of the sickness attacking his master. "It had never been like this. He likes you, miss. Can you help him? Please!"

The last word sounded so anxious that Carrie felt her own heart constrict. She wanted to go running to Jonas and tell him she loved him, but the strong sense of loyalty and discipline in which she had bound herself stopped any such show of weakness.

"No, Johnny, I can't help. I . . . I only wish I could. But you'll find, I'm sure, that Mr. Brandon will be better soon. In a day or so."

"You really think so, miss?" Johnny said woefully. "You really think so?"

"I'm quite sure," she said positively.

He brightened. "Then it is your letter that will make him better." With a sudden skip and a jump he ran off down the road, as if that thought had solved all his problems.

Carrie walked slowly back to the car, her heart as heavy as the tremendous humidity that hung over the island like a thick blanket.

By the time she got back and out of the furnace-like heat of the little car, she was drenched with sweat. She showered and changed, but it seemed to have little effect.

She stood on the verandah, where Mr. Bryant's chair had been moved, and looked in vain for a single breath of wind.

"It's not usual, this time of year," he said, squinting against the sun.

"The weather, you mean?'

"That's right. All topsy-turvy. You'll be feeling the heat badly, no doubt?"

Carrie smiled ruefully. "A bit. I suppose this is what people mean by real tropical heat."

"It's not the heat, but the humidity. We must be in for one hell of a storm. At least that will break it," he told her. "One day I was going to put air-conditioning in the bedrooms, but like all farmers, the land comes before the house."

She turned to him and smiled. "I don't mind, really I don't. When I get back to England I'll only be complaining about the cold."

"We shall miss you," he said gruffly. "Wish we could persuade you to stay."

Carrie opened her mouth to say something neutral, when he went on. "You've decided not to marry my son," he said as a statement and not as a question.

"How did you know?" She looked at him round-eyed.

"Oh, they talk about feminine intuition, but that isn't always right. Perhaps if I'd been on my feet and busy round the place I would never have noticed anything. But here I am, lying, sitting, noticing far more than I should. You ought to be happy and you're not. As each day passes that frown on your pretty forehead gets deeper, as if you wonder how long you can put off telling him. You haven't told him, have you?"

"No," she said in a low voice. "I'm a coward. I want to love him, but what I feel is simply not enough. I felt if I did tell him then I couldn't stay on here, after all your kindness, after the hurt that I shall give Donald."

"Well, you must do as you think, but if you ask me Donald knows too. The boy's not a fool. If things were right you'd both have been running off to the jeweller's to buy a ring. Or is that old-fashioned now?" He smiled at her from under his bushy brows and she saw how Donald would look in another twenty-five years.

Oh, these Bryants were such good people, such kind people. But you couldn't marry because of kindness.

Before she could answer his question Donald came in from the garden. He had stripped off his shirt and wore only a pair of shorts. Even so the heat seemed to be pouring from him.

"God," he said, "I think it's time for a break. The vet hasn't been, then?" he said to his father.

Oliver Bryant shook his head. "No, but he'll only be confirming what we know already, won't he?"

Donald nodded. "Yes, it's swine fever all right." He paused. "You're taking it very calmly, Dad."

The older man shrugged. "It's time for the crying to be over. We have to face facts. We were never meant to make a success of Cinnamon Hill."

Donald scowled. "What do we do? Tell Brandon we've failed—and throw ourselves on his mercy? Oh, no, I'm not beaten yet, because I've got an idea."

"If it needs money Donald, forget it. As a small-holding Cinnamon Hill is finished."

"Maybe, but as a piece of land it isn't. While I've been lying around here, I've done a bit of home-work and a bit of telephoning. Legally, as long as we pay the rent, Brandon can't throw us out."

"So?" His father raised his eyebrows. "How does that help us? We can't live on air."

A slow smile spread over Donald's face. Carrie found herself waiting with clenched hands for something she knew was going to be unpleasant.

"I'm told that if we move fast, and in the right direction, we can have this land made over to some other use—and get paid for it into the bargain. We can spike Brandon's guns yet."

CHAPTER ELEVEN

Carrie realised that in many ways she was an old-fashioned girl. She had always believed that loyalty was something that was just as important as honesty or kindness, or integrity—any of the virtues that a balanced person believed were part of everyday life. If Oliver Bryant had turned to her then and challenged her, she might well have broken down and appealed to them both in her confusion. But he did not. So here she was, with desperate feelings of loyalty, but utterly divided down the middle.

If she kept quiet about this new development, then her betrayal of Jonas would be complete. Yet, if she told him what was happening she could never face any of the Bryants again. Quite apart from her feelings towards Mr. and Mrs. Bryant, she still had a great deal of respect and affection for Donald. How could she possibly let them down?

While her brain was whirling, but getting nowhere, she suddenly realised that Donald was staring at her curiously, speaking to her.

"I'm sorry," she said quickly, "I didn't hear what you said."

"I said, darling," he repeated patiently, "that you had made no comment."

"I . . . I simply didn't know what to say," she returned quickly. "But I do know one thing, that it doesn't seem fair to be going behind someone's back like that. Don't you think that Jonas Brandon would be full of sympathy for what's happened at Cinnamon Hill? Don't you think you ought to give him the *chance* to help?"

"And if he doesn't?" His eyebrows were raised. "No, Carrie, I realise you like the fellow, but you simply don't know him. He'd turn round and laugh in our faces."

Carrie looked at him straight in the eye. "Do you really think he would? Do you think any decent person would do that when faced with people who've worked as hard as your parents have?"

"Whose side are you on?" he snapped.

"I'm not on anyone's side," she protested, with a certain amount of truth. "I'm just asking you to face facts. Besides, if he did turn round and laugh at you, wouldn't that be better than remembering for the rest of your life that you'd stuck a knife in his back!"

Donald looked at her as though he had never seen her before, but before he could say anything, his father put in: "Now look, both of you, it's no good arguing about right or wrong. What's right to one person is wrong to another. We have to think of your mother and Cinnamon Hill. We can't afford to go rushing into anything just to get one up on Brandon."

"I don't want. . . ." Donald started.

"Maybe you don't want," his father returned, "but I don't think your mother will agree to anything that smacks of what she would call 'pulling a fast one'!"

"It would be two to one," Donald argued.

Carrie looked from father to son before she said, "I think it would be better if you two talked about this alone. It really isn't anything to do with me, except I just want everything to be right for Cinnamon Hill."

Donald followed her out under the trees about ten minutes later. She was sitting there on an old wooden seat, her hands clasped about her knees watching the iridescent blue of the sea. She had never seen it quite so flat and calm as it was today—

almost an unnatural flatness. And the heat seemed to be gaining in momentum rather than falling. There was not a breath of wind in the palm trees and as she opened her mouth to seek what air there was it was like swallowing steam from a kettle.

"Is it often like this?" she said, hearing him come up behind her, wanting to stay on neutral ground as long as possible.

"No, hardly ever. We must be in for rain, but even then it's unusual. Still, even rain isn't going to help us much now. Carrie...."

She swung round, unheeding of the question she knew must come. "Donald, please go and talk to Jonas. You both have to live in these islands, so why be enemies? In any case, if you don't go and talk to him, then I think your mother will."

He caught her by the arm. "Don't you mean *you* will?" It was an outright challenge, but before she could face it, he said, "If you do go, it's the end between us. I have to make my own decisions."

"And I have to do what I think is right," she returned. "But one thing is certain, whatever I do I won't go behind your back."

For a moment they faced each other, dangerously near to a real quarrel. Now, said Carrie to herself, now is the time to tell him. But it was as though all the fates were against her, for at that precise moment Ginette appeared to tell him that Miss St Clair was on the telephone—and hovered about until he went inside to take the call.

Afterwards, Carrie thought of that afternoon as the lowest point of her stay on these beautiful islands in the Indian Ocean. She felt utterly bereft as if she were standing on a small piece of land with water washing about her, higher and higher. No one came to help her and yet she did not seem able to help herself. She offered to help Mrs. Bryant in order to try and keep herself occupied, but the older woman refused for once, saying the heat was too much for someone unused to it.

So Carrie swam from the little beach along the road, but as soon as she had come out of the sea she felt as hot as if she had never been in. For a little while she sat under the trees, trying to read a book, but all the time she was intensely aware of the small island only four miles away, today tantalisingly near in the brightness of the sun. What was he doing now? Had he got her note, and what would he think about it? She clenched and unclenched her hands, wondering if her heart was playing her tricks, that Donald could possibly be right about Jonas.

"I love him," she said aloud. "I'm in love with him. Therefore I believe in him." And suddenly she wept for the loss of a love she had glimpsed so briefly.

That night, Carrie learned, was reckoned to be one of the hottest and most humid on record. Everyone seemed to be staring up at the sky as if willing the first drops of rain to fall. But although the air was overladen with moisture, it did not fall, but stayed to encircle everyone and to stifle them.

None of them at Cinnamon Hill slept much, so they were up early the next morning, and because she felt the need to get out of the house Carrie started out on her deliveries before nine o'clock.

It was as she passed the Reef Hotel that the idea came to her, and no sooner did it come than she acted upon it. She stopped the Mini and went into the spacious foyer and asked for Mr. Harvey Mercer. Within five minutes Harvey was walking towards her, hand outstretched in welcome.

"Say, Carrie, this is a nice surprise! I'm just having breakfast. Why not come and have some coffee with me?"

"I'd like to, but I'm working this morning. If I keep the fruit and vegetables in the van for long today I think they'll wilt before I get across the island."

"You could be right there. Even Dad, who's used to heat back home, is up in his room with the air-conditioning full on. And if we have an electricity cut, which appears to be part of island life, I guess there'll be a hotel mutiny. Anyway, it's good to see you, Carrie, because I was going to phone you and and the others to dinner tomorrow. Will you come, and that boy-friend of yours?"

Carrie hesitated, then she realised anything was better than sitting around at Cinnamon Hill in the atmosphere that prevailed at this moment.

"I can't answer for Donald . . . things are a bit tricky on the farm at the moment, but I'd certainly love to come."

"Good. Margo's coming and probably the Raymonds. Can you drop in on them and ask them to confirm?"

Carrie nodded. "Of course, but first. . . ." she hesitated.

He grinned. "I know, I was just realising this wasn't just a social visit to see me. What can I do for you?"

"Harvey, I feel guilty all your kindness, but I have a favour to ask."

"Ask away."

"I want to get to Tern Island this morning. As soon as possible. I don't want to stay, only it's important that I get a message to Jonas and it's the only way I can think of. I suppose I could go down to the harbour and hire a boat, but I don't quite know where to start."

He held up his hand. "Say no more. *Sea Spinner* is yours for the morning. We hadn't planned anything today because of weather. They're all saying there must be a storm so Tern Island is just about as far as I want to go. When do you want to go?"

Carrie glanced at her watch. "I think I can make my rounds in about an hour, if I don't stop and chat. Is that too soon for you?"

"Just right. I'll see you down there in just an hour from now. And don't worry if you're held up—we won't run away."

It was just one hour and ten minutes later that Carrie parked the van on the quayside and boarded *Sea Spinner*. One flick of the engine and Harvey was easing her out of the harbour and towards the reef that lay between the mainland and Tern.

Even at sea there was hardly any more air, but at least what there was seemed slightly dryer.

"You're being very mysterious," Harvey commented, as she joined him at the wheel. "I suppose you're not going to tell me about it?"

"I'd like to," she said honestly, "but it's rather a complicated private problem concerned with the Bryants and their home, Cinnamon Hill."

"Fair enough," he shrugged easily. "But I guess you're hoping that Jonas can fix things."

"In a way. How did you know?"

"Simply because he seems that sort of guy. The strong silent type who people turn to in trouble. An odd character, but I'd trust him a long way."

"You would? I'm ... I'm glad to hear that." Somehow it seemed important to have her own opinion confirmed.

"Sure. But as I say, he's not everyone's cup of tea. Keeps people at arm's length as if he's been kicked in the teeth once too often. I knew someone like that back in the States. It took a rather extraordinary kind of woman to break through the reserve. Anyway, we'll be there in a few minutes. I'm not sure about the tide."

"It's all right, I'll swim the last hundred yards. I always keep a swim-suit in the van. I'll go below and change, if that's all right with you."

He anchored off the spit of land that was now so familiar, and as Carrie dived into the clear water and swam towards it, it was almost as if she were coming home.

Before she reached the shore she saw a figure running along from the huts and recognised Johnny, who was waiting for her as she walked out of the sea. His face cleared as he saw who it was.

"Hello, miss, I thought it was a stranger."

"Hello, Johnny, and what would you have done if I had been a stranger—thrown me off the island?"

He cocked his head on one side, looking doubtful, not quite understanding another sense of humour. "I do not quite know. I would have looked very cross and hoped you would go away."

"And then you would have fetched Mr. Brandon."

"Mr. Brandon is not here."

"Oh." All the tension Carrie had been feeling on the way over seemed to disappear, as if she had been half afraid of meeting him, of asking him if he had come to a decision. She had decided she would say nothing to him of Donald's plans, just humbly ask for his help on behalf of the Bryants.

"He went away this morning, miss. He did not say where he was going, but he looked very much like the thunderclouds that we can see over the mountains."

"You gave him the note?"

"Oh, yes. I hoped it would make him happy, but it did not. No one is able to make my master happy. Perhaps he has gone a long way away."

"I hope not, Johnny," she said quietly, more for

his comfort than her own. "He will never leave Tern."

On the way back, after she had dried and changed, Carrie did not say much, and Harvey, as if he understood her acute disappointment, did not press her for information. He only pointed, as they drew near to land, to the huge clouds gathering over the mountains—just as Johnny had said.

"That sure is going to rain," he remarked. "Ever been in a monsoon before?"

Carrie shook her head.

"It's like a ton of water coming down on you. Quite impossible to keep dry." He looked sideways at her. "Don't look so worried, Carrie, whatever is bugging you can't be quite as bad as that."

She smiled. "I'm sorry, you're quite right—I've just got a lot on my mind. I'm not very good at hiding things."

"You still going back to England at the end of the week?"

"Yes."

"Dad and I will be in London in a few months. Mind if I give you a call?"

Carrie hesitated, not wanting to get involved.

He grinned. "It's all right, no strings attached, I promise. I know you've got your heart hidden somewhere else, but . . . well, I'd just like to see you, talk about the Seychelles. I don't know many people in London, certainly no pretty girls."

"I'd love to see you." Carrie meant what she said. "And if you don't know London well, I'm quite a good guide."

"That's a date, then."

As he spoke the first drops of rain fell and by the time they docked it was sheeting down. They shouted a hurried goodbye with a promise to meet at dinner the following day and then Carrie dived for the shelter of the van. But not before she was as wet as if she had jumped into the sea fully clothed.

She sat for a moment to catch her breath. Mission a failure, but at least she had tried. It looked, from what Johnny said, that Jonas was not prepared to rush and help the Bryants. In her mind Carrie admitted that she was not quite sure what he could do —except not turn them out, but somehow she had hoped that his powers would be greater than any ordinary landlord.

By now the rain was hitting the roof of the car so hard that it sounded like hailstones. She did not dare try to drive, so she waited. It was about twenty minutes before it eased off enough to allow her to make her way slowly and cautiously along the streaming road to Cinnamon Hill.

Carrie was surprised to discover that it was past lunch time, but at least she did not have to offer an explanation for her absence. It was taken for granted that she had been held up by the rain.

"Did you manage to drive all right?" Donald asked her. It was like a question from a stranger. He wasn't looking angry any more, just awkward as though he were uncertain of her.

"Not too bad," she answered, "but I wouldn't like to try and drive when the real rain is coming down."

"You mustn't," he said, "it's much too dangerous."

There was a moment's silence before Carrie said, "I . . . I bumped into Harvey Mercer while I was out. He and his father have asked us and the Raymonds and Margo to dinner at the Reef Hotel tomorrow. You will come, won't you?"

"If you would like to go."

They faced each other again, Carrie smiled rather sadly. "I asked you if *you* wanted to come, Donald. There are only a few more days left and it seemed rather a nice idea to have a small party with Bill and Sally and the Mercers. And Margo. People have been very kind to me while I've been here, but it does seem a bit much at this present time to expect your mother to ask everyone here."

He reached for her hand and held it. "Of course I'll come. It would be good to have a night out anyway and forget our troubles. I . . . I can't believe you're not going to be here next week."

"Nor can I. England is going to seem very cold." She thought he was going to ask her about marrying him. She would have told him the truth this time, she knew she would. But he did not ask, and once again the moment was lost.

It rained all the rest of that day and throughout the night. It stopped for a couple of hours in the morning, then started again before lunch.

In the brief 'dry' period Carrie went out into the garden to breathe the cooler air and listen to the thunder rumbling all round the mountains behind. She looked up at the green-covered hillside that seemed to overhang the whole of Cinnamon Hill. Today—or was it her imagination?—it had a curious air of menace rather than one of friendly shadow. Carrie found herself shivering slightly, not with cold, but because she had seen the other face of these islands, that she had come to love so dearly.

She could only hope that it was not going to rain like this until she left. She wanted to see the far south-west of the island and in particular she wanted to do one of Mahé's most spectacular walks which, according to Sally, led round the coastline to drop down to one of the most beautiful and inaccessible beaches on the island. On the way, she explained, you could see a little group of islands living as they lived almost a century ago, scraping a living from the land about them, but perfectly happy to live in peaceful isolation. They kept a couple of chickens and existed otherwise on the coconuts and the vegetation and the odd fish they could catch.

Carrie dressed carefully for the dinner party that night in her favourite long yellow cotton dress with its scooped neckline and absolutely simple style. She brushed her hair until it had a burnished look, and now that she had been here a fortnight in the sun, her skin had taken on a warm golden look. She looked good, she knew she looked good tonight. If only she had felt happy too, happy enough to gain full enjoyment from the evening ahead.

When she came on to the verandah, the Raymonds were there with Donald because their car had suffered in the rain and simply would not go. In a way she was glad not to be alone with Donald just at the moment.

It was Bill who said, "You look smashing, Carrie, doesn't she, Donald?"

"Yes," said Donald quietly, and gave her a long, slow look.

As Carrie might have guessed, the Mercers did things in stylish informality. Unfortunately the rain prevented the outdoor meal they had planned, but the Reef had set aside part of the open-sided dining-room looking out to sea round a candlelit table for the Mercers' guests, including four strangers, a charming couple from America and two young men from Australia who were so naturally funny that soon the whole party was helpless with laughter. Only when they had had drinks and were sitting down to have the first course about an hour later did Carrie notice that one place at the table nearly opposite her was not occupied.

She drank a little more wine than she usually did and, relaxing, began to enjoy herself. Even Donald appeared to be like his old self. Oh, she was glad he had come! Both of them needed to get out and enjoy themselves.

It was as the waiters cleared away the first course and brought in the plates for the fish that she became aware, listening to one of the young Australians, to whom she was next, of a slight commotion across the table.

Carrie looked up and there, sitting down almost opposite her, was Jonas.

Her eyes were drawn to his as if by a magnet. She opened her mouth and closed it again, as if wanting to speak yet unable to. And though she wanted to look away, she could not. Had she but known it all the naked love in her eyes was there for him to see before she finally forced herself to quench it.

She turned away and said brightly to her neighbour, "That sounds terribly interesting . . . all the way across Australia. I'd love to hear more about it."

And so she put on an eager listening face, but she honestly did not take in a single word he said. She was as deeply aware of Jonas as if he were sitting next to her, holding her.

This is ridiculous, she tried to tell herself, as she clasped her hands tightly together, I've only met him a few times; I'm not even sure I like him—and he's only kissed me once. But of course all that was merely trying to fool herself. She could still feel the imprint of his lips on hers.

There was a subtle change in the dinner party after Jonas arrived. It was as though, without making any effort, he dominated the whole party. When he had first arrived she had felt Donald momentarily stiffen beside her and then, a few moments later, relax, as if he had decided that he was not going to let Jonas Brandon spoil his evening. But even then, he was not quite himself, making her wonder what else he had on his mind.

Some little while later the manager came across and spoke quietly in Donald's ear. Donald pushed back his chair and leaned across to Mr. Mercer.

"I'm awfully sorry, I shall have to leave, there's been a telephone call from my home to say some problem's blown up. Will you forgive me if I go back?"

"Sure, but can we do anything?"

Donald shook his head. "Thanks, but I imagine it's because my mother's on her own, so it's presumably something she can't cope with. I'll try to get back, but if I can't. . . ." he looked across at the Raymonds.

"Don't worry," said Bill, "we'll get a taxi and bring Carrie back, but for heaven's sake, if there's anything I can do, just phone as soon as you get home."

Donald touched Carrie's hand lightly and was gone.

Now she felt even more vulnerable, as if by Donald going like that, he had left some part of her exposed.

"Come on," said Harvey, "we'll take our coffee over on the terrace. The rain has eased off a bit. Besides, they want to clear the main floor for dancing."

"Dancing!" thought Carrie in sudden panic; surely he won't ask me? She did not know how strong she could be once he held her in his arms.

As they moved across to the chairs grouped round a couple of low tables, inevitably Carrie found herself by his side.

"Hello, Carrie."

"Hello." Her voice was very low.

"I got your note from Johnny."

"And are you going to help?" This at least was safe ground.

"I've been thinking about it." His voice to her

172

seemed casual and uncaring.

"That means you aren't going to do anything. Through no fault of their own the Bryants face ruin." She still kept her voice low, but now it was full of intensity.

"And have you planned exactly what I should do for the Bryants?" Those smoky eyes seemed to her to be full of mockery and she could not bear it.

She turned her head quickly away so that he should not see the tears threatening. "I think," she said shakily, "I'll go and have my coffee. This doesn't seem the time or the place to argue about such things." And she moved right across to slip down in the empty chair beside Harvey.

The rest of that evening passed in a blur. She was part of it, laughing and talking, yet right outside, wondering if her heart would split in two. She danced, many times she danced, but never with Jonas, for he did not ask her. And then, about midnight, when thunder was rumbling about the sky again Bill said, "I think we should go, Mr. Mercer, Harvey. The weather sounds as if it's worsening again and there's only the maid with Simon." He turned to Carrie. "If you want to stay. . . ."

But Carrie jumped up. "No, please, I think we should go. I'm worried about the Bryants as well."

"I'll call a taxi . . . if they haven't all gone home on a night like this."

Jonas rose to his feet. "Don't do that, Bill. I'm going to drop Margo home, and your place and Cinnamon Hill are only a few miles out of my way."

Goodbyes were brief, for there were dashes into the car to beat the rain. Fortunately Bill got in front with Jonas to make room for the three girls in the back. Margo and the Raymonds talked happily about the evening all the way home, not noticing that neither Carrie nor Jonas joined in.

They reached the foot of Cinnamon Hill to find that the whole rough track was a torrent of water.

"You'll never get the car up there," said Bill. "I'm afraid, Carrie you're going to get wet, but if you can wait two shakes I'll go into our place and get an umbrella."

But Carrie shook her head ruefully. "I don't honestly think that will make much difference. My dress is cotton, it won't hurt, and my shoes . . . well, they and my feet will dry."

"Then I'll come up with you," said Bill. "Look, there's Mrs. Bryant coming out of the house. What on earth is she doing that for?"

"I think," said Jonas crisply, "something must be wrong. You two girls stay in the car for a moment while Bill and I investigate. They're probably flooded out."

He backed the car on to the sea side of the road, in what little shelter there was. It was as he opened the door that everything seemed to happen. Afterwards, Carrie felt that the whole terrible drama was played out in slow motion.

There was an enormous rumble which they all took to be thunder, only it was not thunder but the side of the hillside above the house splitting in two. With an even louder roar the whole hill seemed to be on the move, crashing, pounding, tumbling, and they were all forced to stand there, appalled, watching the pig unit disappear and then the whole white house, cracking and groaning as the weatherboard snapped like matchwood.

Carrie hid her face in her hands, unable to look any more. "Oh, no!" she cried. "No, please!" and then suddenly all was silence, except for the rushing of water.

Jonas took charge immediately. "Sally, go into your place and get Simon out, just in case there's more trouble. Then somehow get to a phone or stop a car and tell the police. And you'd better contact the hospital as well." And then he started to run with Bill following him and the two girls not far behind.

Half way up the shattered hillside Mrs. Bryant was crouching not far from where they had seen her. The landslide had somehow passed her by. But she was staring stricken at the pile of rubble.

"Mrs. Bryant," said Jonas, "are you all right? And where are the others?"

"I'm all right," she said dully, "and my husband is too. Somehow he was thrown out over there, and though I can't move him, I don't think he's hurt. It's Donald. . . ."

It was Margo who said shrilly, "Where's Donald?"

"He was inside. He must be somewhere under the house." And Mrs. Bryant started to weep silently.

CHAPTER TWELVE

Within the next few minutes Mrs. Bryant and her husband—who was, miraculously, only bruised— were taken, along with young Simon, to a near neighbour whose house was on the coastal side of road. Sally said she would stay with them and be responsible for keeping them informed with news.

Mrs. Bryant wanted to stay and help the others, but it was quite obvious that she was in a state of shock and needed to be somewhere warm and dry.

Somehow everyone had turned up to help and soon the devastated area was ringed with a mixture of electric lamps and flares. At least the rain had stopped so, although the hazard of further falls was not entirely gone, at least it was lessened considerably.

While all the preparations were being made Bill and Jonas started to crawl cautiously over the rubble to what remained of the house.

Carrie and Margo stood together, holding each other tightly, the same fear in both their hearts, believing there could be only one answer.

It was Margo who voiced their fears at last. "I think we have to realise, Carrie, that the chances of anyone being alive in all that are very small." Although she spoke clearly, the voice was so strange it did not sound like Margo at all.

"If only I'd gone back with him!"

"And then there would have been two of you!" That was more like the old Margo.

Carrie started up to where the two men could just be seen crawling up the slope. "He must be all right," she said fiercely. "Donald is strong. He must have a chance." She wanted to cry, but the whole disaster seemed so enormous that she was almost beyond tears.

"I'm not very good at praying," said Margo, "but I think at this moment I want very badly to learn."

And so the two girls stood there, heads bowed, each silent with her own desperate plea for help.

It was almost at that moment that they heard Bill's yell. "He's alive! He's alive!" And a great cry went up from all those who had gathered, wanting to help, but waiting for instructions.

A few moments later Jonas and Bill came down and consulted with the small band of policemen who had turned up. But it was still, Carrie noted with surprise, Jonas who was in charge.

"I think," he said, "one side of the fall is fairly stable. There are no rocks and the main body of earth has come away in the direction of the hillside's tilt, so if we're careful we should be able to remove at least the wood and plaster that's covering him. As far as I can gather he doesn't think he's seriously hurt, but he's trapped and totally unable to move. Something in the nature of a beam is across him and holding up all the heavier stuff that could have smothered him. I suggest we form a chain in twos so that too many are not standing on dangerous ground and start to move what rubble we can."

As dawn came up over the eastern sky they were still digging. They had hardly stopped all night, except each man to take a short rest. It was a long and painfully hard job, for it was obvious that with the delicate balance holding Donald away from death that no heavy equipment could be brought in to help.

Both Margo and Carrie had also hardly moved from the scene except to go down to give news to the Bryants and make coffee and cool drinks to bring up to the men working. Since that earlier time they had hardly spoken, mainly because they were both too tense to allow any expression of feelings.

At some moment after sunrise when steam was coming off the sodden ground, the work up the hillside suddenly stopped, and the men seemed to be staring at the place they had cleared. Then gradually they all came down to the flatter ground where the girls and other onlookers were waiting patiently.

"What's happening?" asked Carrie eagerly. "He is still all right, isn't he?"

Jonas nodded. "At the moment," he said soberly, "but we've run into some difficulty. We've dug as far as we can go, but if we move anything else the whole lot will come crashing down. We have to decide what to do next."

Carrie looked at his tired face, covered with dirt and filth, and wondered how she could ever have had any doubts about his honour. He had worked here for more than five hours desperately trying to save the life of a man who was not even his friend, never stinting himself.

For the next few moments the men there argued back and forth, obviously not reaching any conclusions until suddenly Jonas stepped out of the circle once more.

"We have only one choice, when it comes down to it," he said sharply.

"And what's that?" asked Bill.

"Someone has to go in and bring him out. *I'll* go in and bring him out."

Carrie heard Bill's sharply indrawn breath. "If you do that, Jonas, you have only a fifty-fifty chance of getting out yourself."

"It's a chance I'm prepared to take."

"No," said Bill again. "Somehow we can get some grappling equipment up here. There must be a way of doing it."

Jonas turned to him and answered dryly. "Yes, and by that time the rest of that slide will go and cover all that we've done this morning. *You* saw that, Bill. And if it does happen then Donald won't stand a chance."

Bill was silent and Carrie knew that Jonas must be speaking the truth.

As if he knew she was looking at him, Jonas suddenly turned and met Carrie's eyes. She knew there was a plea in them, but whether it was that he should go in and try to save Donald, or whether he should think of his own life first, Carrie could not have said. She only knew he gave her the briefest of smiles, one last hard look, almost as if he were trying to engrave her face on his memory. Then he had turned on his heel, barked a few instructions to the men about him, and started to scramble up the hill again.

Carrie said in a low voice, "I know I'm a coward, but I can't stand here and watch. I feel if I do some of my fears could reach out to them. I . . . I'm going across the road to sit by the boathouse. I'll hear soon enough that something has happened."

Margo nodded. Then she said suddenly, "Carrie, tell me one thing. And I want the truth."

Carrie waited.

"You're in love with Jonas, aren't you?"

With the briefest of nods and a blinding curtain of tears, Carrie turned on her heel to cross the road.

Already the sun's heat was strong enough to dry the sand, but yesterday's heavy, unbearable humidity had gone. She gazed out across the sea as she had done so often in the past two weeks and wondered how so much joy and happiness could change to this terror. Her own problems—oh, how foolish they seemed now! Nevertheless, in one way she was glad she had not told Donald of her decision. He

179

could be lying there now, thinking about it.

She did not know how long she went on sitting there, but through sheer exhaustion she must have fallen asleep. The first thing she knew was a tap on the shoulder from Margo.

She jerked up, her eyes blind with panic.

"They're safe," said Margo, "both of them."

Only then did Carrie burst into tears.

Donald was carried into the Raymonds' house which was the nearest and put to bed there after the doctor had examined him. He had suffered no real injury except extensive cuts and bruises and a sprained wrist, along with some lacerations to his head. What he needed now, the doctor said, was a long sleep.

His mother had arrived on the scene and with Carrie and Margo on either side of her she watched Donald being carried across on a stretcher.

He managed a grin at all of them. "See, you can't get rid of me so easily!"

Carrie looked around for Jonas. She wanted to say thank you; to express her deep admiration for his courage, but when she asked Bill where he was, Bill looked about him in surprise. "I don't know; he was here a few minutes ago. Typical of the man, though, to disappear before anyone can praise him, or thank him." He turned to Carrie. "You look exhausted too. Are you going to come back with us for a shower and a sleep?"

Before Carrie could answer, Margo put in: "No, she'll come back with me, Bill. You've got enough on your plate with the Bryants. We'll come back this afternoon."

They were given a lift into town in a police car, and only after Margo said that she would find Carrie a change of clothes did Carrie realise that she had lost all her possessions except her handbag and her long yellow dress. But the Bryants would have even less. Now that everyone was safe there was all this worry to contemplate. She said as much to Margo.

"I suppose you've lost your passport," the other girl said.

"Oddly, no," Carrie answered wryly, "it's one of those things I always keep in my handbag. Even my ticket is clipped in there. But Mrs. Bryant . . . poor Mrs. Bryant!"

After coffee and rolls at the Casuarina, she slept for most of the day until the sun had started to dip in the sky. She found there were washing things on her bed and a crisp cotton dress. Her underwear had been washed and pressed.

She found Margo in the office. "Thank you," she said simply. "And did you manage to sleep?"

"Enough. After you've had something to eat I thought we'd drive back to the Raymonds'. Would you like that?"

"Oh, yes."

When they stopped outside the Raymonds' Carrie looked up towards what had been Cinnamon Hill. She was surprised and disturbed to see Mrs. Bryant standing looking at the ruins of her home.

Impulsively she said to Margo, "You go in and keep Donald company for a moment. I must just have a word with Mrs. Bryant."

She walked up to where the older woman was standing, expecting sorrow, even tears. But the woman before her had a bearing as proud as ever and the smile she gave Carrie was not one of misery.

Instinctively Carrie flung herself into those warm, motherly arms. "Oh, I'm so sorry, so dreadfully sorry. Could anything worse have happened?"

"Yes, dear, it could. Donald could have died. That's when I realized I had to count my blessings."

"But . . . but you've got nothing left, nothing at

181

all."

"We've got our health and strength. Oliver will be up and about soon and then together we'll start again. I think it may be even rather fun."

Carrie looked at her in amazement. "I think you're . . . you're marvellous!"

"No, just practical. That's always been my strength. I always remember as a child my mother telling me that only a fool ever looked backward. And she was quite right. Besides, there is some good that has come out of all this."

"And what's that?" Carrie was now unbelieving.

"Some time very early this morning, when he was having a short break, Jonas Brandon came over to see me. Partly to reassure me that Donald was all right, but also to tell me a decision he had taken about Cinnamon Hill right from the beginning."

"Go on," said Carrie quietly.

"Well, he said he knew that whatever we did we could never make this place into the success our hard work deserved. But you know, Oliver picked this piece of land, and nothing would make him change his mind. There was another piece, also belonging to Jonas, a little further south, but Oliver wouldn't hear of it. Too much off the beaten track, he said—oh, and various other criticisms. Well, apparently Jonas never did anything with that piece of land because he knew it was meant for some kind of farming, its soil being more fertile than usual for Mahé. As soon as he saw our difficulties—long before we saw them ourselves, I suspect—he started clearing that land and fertilising it. I always knew people misjudged him. He has the interests of these islands completely at heart, and more than anything else he wants to make the Seychelles more self-sufficient. He says we're the only people who can farm that land successfully. He says if we agree to work for him for the first couple of years then he'll let us have it at a good price. I suspect that's so that we won't have to raise capital yet."

"And will Mr. Bryant agree?" Carrie asked.

"I think so. We talked about it today. It would have been his pride that would have stopped him, but after all, Jonas did save Donald's life, so we both have to learn humility some time. So the future is not quite so black as it seems."

"Oh, I'm glad," said Carrie, "so glad."

"Thank you for your good wishes." Mrs. Bryant bent to kiss her. "And now you must go and see Donald."

"Yes." Carrie paused. "I'm afraid I have to tell you that I'm not going to marry him."

"I know, my husband told me. But if you ever come back, you will still be as my daughter. Remember that, Carrie."

Carrie nodded, her heart too full to speak, then turned to make her way back to the Raymonds' bungalow.

Sally was in the garden trying to patch up some of the damage the storm had caused to her plants. "Go in," she said. "Donald knows you're here."

In the rubber sandals Carrie had borrowed, her feet made no sound as she went into the open door and hesitated, wondering in which room Donald was. It was as she hesitated that she heard the voices, and while she would not normally have listened—eavesdropped, she reminded herself—she simply could not stop herself.

". . . I should never have been so stupid as to leave you. . . ." Margo was saying.

"Maybe, but we met too soon—too soon for you—after Hugh's death. You didn't want to fall in love with anyone. And I was fool enough to think it was Jonas."

"Like chalk and cheese," she said in a soft, wry voice. And then, "Oh, God, Donald, I've been such a fool!"

"So have I, Margo, but what are we going to do? What are we going to do?"

Carrie tiptoed away. This was the last thing she had expected—or was it? On her arrival at Cinnamon Hill she had been suspicious, but somehow as Donald kept pressing her to marry him, most of those suspicions had been allayed.

At that moment Carrie made one of the swiftest decisions she had ever made in her life. The time was over for beating around the bush. Making as much noise as she should, she came to the front door and called: "Margo . . . Donald . . . are you there?"

A moment's silence and then: "We're here, Carrie," and Margo appeared in an open doorway. She did not look at all flustered, but Carrie noticed there were signs of strain round her eyes.

Donald was in bed with his wrist in plaster and a bandage over his head. Otherwise, apart from a faintly guilty look, he did not seem as if he had gone through what he had last night.

Carrie bent to kiss him on the cheek, and squeeze his good hand. "Hello, Donald, thank God you're safe."

"I was lucky," he said and then, with a certain amount of dryness in his voice. "And of course, I have Jonas Brandon to thank."

"You . . . you know he's given your parents a new deal over Cinnamon Hill?"

He nodded, then shrugged. "I suppose I shall have to start revising my thinking about him. That doesn't mean we have to become great pals all of a sudden!"

"Of course not!" But Carrie's heart was lighter and she saw that Margo was hiding a smile. She stood

184

up suddenly. "Donald, I think there's something I should say to you. I know it isn't a very good moment, but I've discovered there isn't such a thing as the right moment."

Margo moved swiftly. "I'll go."

"No, please stay. It's private in a way, but I think Donald will understand. I . . . I decided that I don't think it would be right for us to get married."

"Carrie. . . ."

"No, wait, let me finish, it's difficult enough as it is. I think I did love you, in a way I still do, but it's not enough for marriage. We think too differently. Since I've been over here, I've discovered quite a lot about myself. Perhaps I'm not ready for marriage, but whatever it is, please, Donald, tell me that I'm right."

"Yes," he said slowly, "I suppose you are. There's something missing, isn't there, but then this is why you came to stay over here. I'm glad you came, Carrie."

"So am I," she said simply, and meant it. In the doorway she paused. "I'll stay at Margo's, Donald, but I'll see you before I go. There are only three days left now. Take care." And she slipped out before either of them could stop her.

Well, it was done, and it was like a weight off her mind. She knew she would never reveal to either of them what she had overheard. She guessed that neither Margo nor Donald would say anything about themselves in the next three days, but some time after she had gone they would get married quietly. It might be a stormy marriage, but she felt it was probably the right one.

Now she had to look forward to going home and starting again. She had certainly burnt her boats with Jonas, but it was too late to change all that. She knew by the way he spoke to her last night, the way he had walked away, that he had cut her out of his life as easily as he had pulled her into it.

Somehow the next day slipped by, what with shopping and helping Margo and seeing the last of the island, although even the joy had gone out of that now. There was a suppressed happiness about Margo, a new spring in her step, and Carrie longed to wish her happiness, but she knew that would have to wait until she heard officially in England and could write a letter.

It was after lunch the following day when she had been swimming down in the little bay below the Casuarina and had just dried off when she heard the call behind her. "Miss, oh, please, miss!" And there was young Johnny, but this time there was no beaming smile, only a face as mournful as a funeral.

"What's the matter, Johnny?"

"It's the master, he is not well. Please to come and help."

"I can't help, Johnny—if he's not well, then you must get a doctor."

"Oh, miss, I have tried, but they cannot come till later. All are busy. I am afraid to be left alone with him."

"Then we'll find Miss St Clair. Come along." And she went purposefully up towards the hotel to look for Margo.

"Miss St Clair not there. No one is there. Please, miss, you must help me!"

He was quite right, there was no one there.

"And you say the doctor is coming later?"

The boy nodded.

Carrie hesitated. This was none of her business, and Jonas would not thank her for arriving unasked for on Tern. And yet her heart was hammering and the boy was looking so pitiful that she could not possibly turn her back. What if Jonas was really ill and

186

there was no one there with him? Well, she told herself, she supposed she would do it for anyone.

"Wait," she said to Johnny. "I'll get dressed, but better still bring your boat round here."

The smile was back, like a beacon, and he dashed off.

The narrow pirogue seemed to skim over the calm water. With a boat like this there were no problems with coral or shallow water, so they went direct to the island.

As the familiar outline drew nearer Carrie felt her heart begin to hammer again. It was as if she were coming home. But of course that was just an illusion.

Johnny beached the boat. "You go there, miss, I will arrange the boat."

She turned towards the hut and as she drew near she started to run. If he were really ill. . . .

"Hello, Carrie."

She stopped suddenly. He was sitting on an old chair, whittling away at a piece of wood as if he were merely amusing himself. He looked as healthy as she had even seen him.

"You're supposed to be ill!" she accused him.

"There are all kinds of illness."

She did not understand. "Then why did Johnny bring me here?"

"Because I asked him to. He enjoys a bit of play-acting."

She stood stiffly in front of him. "If that's your idea of a joke, I don't find it very funny. I suppose you want to tell me how decent you've been to the Bryants, crow a little and then send me back. Well, thank you very much, I'd prefer to go now. Perhaps you would tell Johnny that too."

"Certainly not. Now that I've got you here I'm not getting rid of you as easily as that." She thought

187

he was laughing at her, but could not be sure. "Besides, I wanted to test a theory. It worked."

"I would have come to anyone who was ill," she said coldly.

"What—without nursing experience?" He patted the chair beside him. "Sit down, Carrie, we've got a lot to talk about."

"Have we? About what?"

"Mainly our wedding. I'm not very good at that kind of thing, but if you want a bit of fuss I'm prepared to give in gracefully."

Now she really thought she must be dreaming. "Please, Jonas," she said shakily, "don't play with me."

"I'm not," He pulled her down beside him. "I've never been more serious in my life." Suddenly he was no longer laughing. "I love you, Carrie, right from the beginning I knew we were meant for each other, but—well, you had to work a few things out. Now you've done those, so there's nothing in our way. You can go home to England tomorrow, sort out your affairs, then I shall come and fetch you."

"You seem to have it all worked out," she whispered.

"Oh, I have. I had almost from the beginning. There's only one thing missing."

"What's that?"

"I'm sure of myself, utterly sure, but suddenly I'm not so sure about you."

"I love you, Jonas, is that what you want me to say?"

He smiled and she thought it was the most marvellous smile she had ever seen.

"Now it's all fine." And he pulled her into his arms.

Golden Harlequin $1.95 per vol.
Each Volume Contains 3 Complete Harlequin Romances

☐ ## Volume 20

DOCTOR SARA COMES HOME by Elizabeth Houghton   (#594)
After an unfortunate mishap, Sara Lloyd, a brilliant doctor went to live for a year in the delightful but remote Welsh Mountains. Coming to terms with life again, she found Robert Llewellyn becoming a very dear friend, then, suddenly, out of her "hidden" past walked — Stephen Grey.

THE TALL PINES by Celine Conway   (#736)
Bret was deeply involved in chemical research in Western Canada. The last thing he needed on his mind was this pale, fragile English girl, and her foolishly quixotic mission. The "last thing" soon became the most important part of his whole life . . .

ACROSS THE COUNTER by Mary Burchell   (#603)
Katherine was assigned to re-organize one of Kendales' departments in the Midlands. Within a week, she became engaged to Paul Kendale while she still loved someone else — it wasn't the shop, but her own life which underwent the greatest change . . .

☐ ## Volume 21

THE DOCTOR'S DAUGHTERS by Anne Weale   (#716)
When the new squire arrived at Dr. Burney's busy and pleasant household, his presence became a disturbing influence on the lives of all the doctor's family. It was the eldest daughter, Rachel, who quickly found that Daniel Elliot was not a man to be ignored:

GATES OF DAWN by Susan Barrie   (#792)
Richard Trenchard was accustomed to having his own way, not least with women. This applied even to his sister, and to her secretary, Melanie Brooks, who fell victim to Richard's power. But, in the end, was it Richard, or Melanie, who really did have their way?

THE GIRL AT SNOWY RIVER by Joyce Dingwell   (#808)
Upon arrival in Australia, Prudence found herself the only girl among 400 men! To most women, this would have been heavenly. But, what if the most important of these men is determined to get rid of you — as was precisely the case . . .

Golden Harlequin $1.95 per vol.

Each Volume Contains 3 Complete Harlequin Romances

☐ Volume 25

DOCTOR MEMSAHIB by Juliet Shore   (#531)
Mark Travers had little use for a woman plastic surgeon in his hospital in Bengal, but the Rajah had requested her, so he might make use of her visit. An accusing, anonymous letter had preceded Ruth's arrival, and try as he did, Mark could not quite put it out of his head . . .

AND BE THY LOVE by Rose Burghley   (#617)
"Is it necessary to know all there is to know about a man or woman before falling in love with him or her?" When Caroline was asked this question, her answer came easily. It was later that she would have cause to weigh the value of these words . . .

BLACK CHARLES by Esther Wyndham   (#680)
A man who would never marry! Whose character was arrogant and fierce! He was the one dark haired male born of this generation into the Pendleton family, and alas, it was the fate of young Audrey Lawrence to cross swords with — Black Charles Pendleton.

☐ Volume 27

SANDFLOWER by Jane Arbor   (#576)
Both girls were named Elizabeth. Roger Yate thought Liz to be forceful and courageous, and Beth, sweet appealing little Beth. In his opinion of the characters of these two girls, the brilliant young doctor could not have been more wrong!

NURSE TRENT'S CHILDREN by Joyce Dingwell   (#626)
A tragic accident had ended Cathy's training, so she came to Australia as housemother to a number of orphaned children. Dr. Jeremy Malcolm seemed to take an immediate dislike to her organization, and more particularly, to Cathy herself.

INHERIT MY HEART by Mary Burchell   (#782)
The only way left for Mrs. Thurrock and her daughter Naomi to share the inheritance now, was for Naomi to marry Jerome. It might have been a good idea, if only Naomi hadn't infinitely preferred his brother, Martin . . .

Golden Harlequin $1.95 per vol.
Each Volume Contains 3 Complete Harlequin Romances

☐ Volume 31

THE HOUSE ON FLAMINGO CAY by Anne Weale (#743)
Angela Gordon was glamorous and ambitious, and confident that in the Bahamas she would find herself a rich husband. The wealthy Stephen Rand was perfect, but alas — he was much more attracted by her sister Sara's quieter charms ...

THE WEDDING DRESS by Mary Burchell (#813)
Loraine could hardly contain herself, she was going from the seclusion of an English boarding school, straight into the heady atmosphere of Paris, in May. Her only concern was, her unknown guardian — and his plans for her ...

TOWARDS THE SUN by Rosalind Brett (#693)
There was a warm loveliness all around her on the sun-soaked South Sea island of Bali, yet, Sherlie was miserable. She was exploited by a chilly stepmother and even worse, she fell in love with the totally inaccessible — Paul Stewart.

☐ Volume 32

DOCTOR'S ASSISTANT by Celine Conway (#826)
Laurette decided that Charles Heron was an autocrat, who thought far too much of himself. She also knew that she meant absolutely nothing in his life — a suitable situation? Quite, — until she realized, that for the very first time, she was in love!

TENDER CONQUEST by Joyce Dingwell (#854)
Bridget found her work fascinating. She loved travelling around, meeting and talking to all sorts of people, who all seemed to enjoy talking to her. All, except the new Market Research Manager, who considered her quite inefficient.

WHEN YOU HAVE FOUND ME by Elizabeth Hoy (#526)
During the crossing to Ireland, Cathleen offered to take care of a small kitten. A friendly gesture, which had some far reaching consequences, leading her to some very strange — and exciting results!